AFTER THE WORST THING HAPPENS

AFTER THE WORST THING HAPPENS

Audrey Vernick

MARGARET FERGUSON BOOKS
HOLIDAY HOUSE • NEW YORK

Margaret Ferguson Books

Printed and bound in March 2020 at Maple Press, York, PA, USA.
www.holidayhouse.com
First edition
1 3 5 7 9 10 8 6 4 2

Library of Congress Cataloging-in-Publication Data

Names: Vernick, Audrey, author.
Title: After the worst thing happens / Audrey Vernick.
Description: First edition. | New York : Holiday House, [2020] | Audience: Ages 9–12. | Audience: Grades 4–7. | Summary: Twelve-year-old Army is reeling after her thoughtlessness leads to her dog's death, but channels her grief into a plan to help keep the new neighbors' autistic daughter from wandering away.
Identifiers: LCCN 2019025603 | ISBN 9780823444908 (hardcover)
Subjects: CYAC: Neighbors—Fiction. | Autism—Fiction. | Grief—Fiction. Dogs—Therapeutic use—Fiction. | Family life—New Jersey—Fiction. New Jersey—Fiction.
Classification: LCC PZ7.V5973 Aft 2020 | DDC [Fic]—dc23
LC record available at https://lccn.loc.gov/2019025603

For Liz Garton Scanlon, who willed this book into being, and in loving memory of Hootie, a very good dog.

AFTER THE WORST THING HAPPENS

CHAPTER ONE

When I was little and woke from a bad dream, I'd climb out of bed and walk through the dark hallway to my parents' room. I would push the door open silently and stand there in the blackness, staring at where I knew my mother was sleeping. Before long, she'd wake up and get out of bed and lead me to my room. She'd listen while I told her about the monster or quicksand or swampy lake that had scared me until I fell back asleep.

I never knew how to explain why my mom would wake up just because I was standing there looking at her in the darkness. I guess I thought it was some kind of magic.

These days *I'm* the one who gets stared awake. By my dog, my perfect dog, Maybe.

He doesn't make a sound. Doesn't even move. But in the morning, Maybe stares me awake from his bed. I know now it's not magic, but what is it? A link, a bond? It must be some invisible thread that connects us.

And as much as I love to sleep, especially under piles of blankets, I never mind being wakened by sweet Maybe. He is a fluffy little white mop of love, who wakes up, stays still, and stares. When I finally look his way, he starts stamping his front two paws with impatience until I swing my feet from bed to floor. Then he bursts from his bed to help me start the day, tail wagging with excitement. Once I reach for the leash, he has a helicopter tail going, full circles. Pure joy.

So even though I wasn't born a morning person, I love our seven-thirty walks around the block. It's Monday and early in October. Leaves have just started to fall from trees, but it doesn't feel like autumn. This year, the warm weather is holding on for dear life and as a summer lover, I am completely in favor of this.

We cross to the other side of the street and I hear Mrs. Rooney calling my name.

"Army, sweetheart, can you come here for just a minute?" Maybe and I meet her on the patch of curb grass in front of her house. She bends down and pets Maybe.

I've been helping her and Mr. Rooney pack up their house into boxes. They have so much *stuff*. There is no way anyone on this earth has as much stuff as they do. "I wanted to give you these," she says, placing a pair of soft red mittens in my hand. "Though it's been so warm, it's hard to imagine it'll ever be cold in New Jersey again."

Even before I helped Mrs. Rooney pack, she used to invite me over for tea and cookies and ask me to help ball her yarn. I'd sit facing her, the skein of wool stretched between my two hands, while she rolled it into a ball. Her grandkids live in Maine, where she's moving now, and she knits for them all the time.

"I thought these were for Addie," I say.

Mrs. Rooney shrugs in a guilty-looking way and says, "I lied." And then she laughs.

She pulls me close to her and says, "You think of me when you wear those mittens and promise me you won't feel bad when you lose one, because that's the thing with mittens. You will lose one. Just keep the other as a memory of me. And our lovely afternoons together."

Mrs. Rooney and I already said goodbye yesterday, so this is especially hard. A second goodbye. "Thank you," I say. "I'll miss you."

"And I will miss you, Army. Thanks for being such a good neighbor."

I might start crying but Maybe tugs on the leash and I really do need to get this walk done so I can get ready for school before the bus comes. We head around the corner to Mr. Hoffart's house. The newspaper's waiting, as it always is, at the top of his sloping driveway. I pick it up and fast-walk to his front door, where I leave it for him, next to the giant wire reindeer that has become an all-seasons decoration the last couple of years.

Mr. Hoffart's kind of old and very wobbly and I'm almost sure he has won an award for walking more slowly than any other person on earth has ever walked. He was a slow walker *before* he broke his ankle on a patch of ice last winter, and it always makes me nervous to think of the slow walk he has to take all the way to the top of his driveway—which isn't only uphill, but kind of bumpy with cracks too. And then—even worse—back down to his house. So Maybe and I bring his paper to his front door every morning.

He has no idea it's me. I like being a secret part of his everyday life.

We head home, where I grab a breakfast bar from the pantry, thinking about doing all the usual stuff—shower, double-check backpack for homework, make lunch, avoid Maybe's eyes. If it were up to Maybe, I would never leave the house without him. I would be homeschooled, homebound, home-everythinged.

This morning my parents, who have to meet with a subcontractor all the way out in Orangeboro, dropped my nine-year-old brother, Navy, at school early, because he needs extra help with math. So I'm home alone, which doesn't happen often enough.

I get ready fast so I can do my favorite thing that I will never admit is my favorite thing because it's something I started doing when I was six and perhaps not the most mature thing a girl twice that age should still be doing. When no one is around, Maybe and I play wild animal race in the hall. I get down on all fours and chase him and let him chase me and sometimes Maybe gets so excited he starts barking and can't stop and that's usually when I go grab one of his favorite treats from the orange tin next to the fridge to quiet him.

It's silly and ridiculous and one of the most fun things ever because I manage to not think about anything but being an animal. I wonder if that's why my connection to Maybe is so strong—because I get down on all fours with him whenever I can.

And now he's racing with his ropy ZippyPaws dog in his mouth, and he flies upstairs and he's faster than me, which is ridiculous because how can a body so little move so fast? But I race him into my room and he stands at my bed, drops ZippyPaws dog, and barks.

"What?" I ask. Like he's going to answer.

He waits for me to understand. I look on the bed. A mess, and a reminder to make it, so thank you, Maybe. What else? I look under the bed, which is so awful that if my mother ever looked there she might . . . I can't even imagine, honestly.

But Maybe's never wrong. He barks for a reason. Today's reason: tennis ball, wedged into an old sneaker under my bed. It barely fits in his mouth, but he trots away and our game is over, no need for orange-tin treats. I get my stuff together and walk to the corner to wait for the school bus.

I watch Mr. and Mrs. Rooney taking pictures of each other in front of their house.

CHAPTER TWO

There are things I *have* to do and things I *want* and *love* to do. Today after school is unfortunately one of those have-to-do times. Whenever my parents are busy with work, I have to get off the middle school bus near Clay Coves Elementary school to pick up my brother, Navy, and bring him home. It's not a perfect situation—my bus takes forever, so sometimes I'm a little late, but Navy doesn't seem to mind waiting in the library.

I'm almost at the entrance when I see two men and three dogs walk into the school. Which is bizarre. My brain quickly thinks about and then rejects some police or bomb thing—those two men were not moving quickly, and there aren't any cop cars in the lot.

But the oddness of this—the impossibility of it. Dogs! Walking into Clay Coves Elementary like they're third graders or something.

I should turn left and go get Navy from the library, but I follow the dogs instead. I can't help it.

They are hilarious from behind. One's a golden retriever

whose tail, with its long, plumy fur, wags very slowly back and forth.

The one in the middle is mostly white with big black spots. She has a boxy, muscly body that doesn't look friendly, but the way she walks—on her toes, if she could do that—makes her seem like she's trying out her ballerina skills.

And the one lagging behind is just a bundle of white fur, with these great legs that belong on a Muppet, a much bigger version of Maybe.

The men walk the dogs into the gym, where they are greeted by Navy's Cub Scout pack leader, Rob. The gym is a buzzing room of energy, with Scouts racing and jumping and screaming like wild things.

Shoot! No one told me about a Scouts meeting today. Or did I forget? I find Navy in the crowd of boys but before I can even finish saying, "Why didn't you tell me there was a meeting so I'd come later?" he's whining, "Please? I'm sorry, I forgot! They added an extra one because it's a special presentation. I need to stay."

I probably wouldn't be so nice if there weren't three fantastic dogs in the gym. In the *gym.* I don't have a choice anyway, so I say okay and he rejoins the wild-thing races.

The dogs follow the men to the front and without even being told, sit. It's hard to believe how calm they are while dozens of boys race around, tagging one another, changing direction unexpectedly, sneakers squeaking, squeaks echoing. I wonder what Maybe would do—I have a feeling he'd be acting more like the Scouts than like the well-behaved dogs: running in circles, mouth open wide in a big panting grin.

"Army?" A girl's voice? In the ripe-with-Boy-Scouts-smell elementary school gym? Oh God, no. Elsie Jenkins. That's her all right, dressed completely in tan like she always is. I don't know her well, just as the girl who never stops talking when she's called on in Language Arts. For some unknown reason, my best friend JennaLouise and I always use both her first and last names.

"Why are you here?" I ask, before realizing how rude that sounds.

Navy zips by and sticks his index finger in, hard, above my waist, something he figured out long ago bugs me like crazy. I want to put my hand on the back of his head and give it a good push. "That's my brother," I say with all the joy you can imagine comes with such a statement.

Rob raises his hand to get the boys' attention. "Scouts, eyes up front."

There's a big groan. Rob whistles. "Our guests are ready. I need you to sit quietly right here," he says, pointing.

The boys aren't quiet, but they do flop down in a sloppy-looking blob on the floor.

Elsie Jenkins keeps looking at me. I try not to squirm. "Which one's your brother?" I ask.

"Huh?" she asks. "Oh. I don't have brothers. Or sisters. I'm just babysitting Grayson—over there." She points at the clump of boys.

"Oh, I know Grayson," I say, because I do. And because it's the only thing I can think of to say to Elsie Jenkins.

She walks to the chairs set up at the side of the gym. She looks back, maybe expecting me to follow, but I sit down on the floor where I am, behind the Scouts.

"We are from Service with a Wag and we train dogs to help people," one of the men says. "My name is Bill Chaplain, and this is my head trainer, Fred Jarvison. We're going to talk to you today about the work we do and the work our dogs do. Basically, we train service dogs to assist people who need help in their daily lives."

As the man talks, the other shows all the things the dogs can do. These dogs! They are so well trained, doing everything they're told without even pausing, and sometimes doing things just because they know. Like anytime Fred walks a dog, the minute he stops, the dog just sits. Automatically. Like a robot dog.

Then the men run through exercises where the dogs push a small wheelchair and press a button to turn a light off. They say some of their dogs can tell when people are about to have a seizure and then alert someone. How is that possible?

It's so impressive even the Cub Scouts are quiet!

The men talk about how rewarding their work is. How not too many people think about training service dogs as a career, but it's deeply satisfying to help people this way. That volunteers can help by serving as foster families, caring for puppies when they're little—training and socializing them, taking them to all kinds of places to get them used to different settings. The more specialized skills, like the ones the dogs just performed for us, are taught by certified trainers once the puppies have been returned to Service with a Wag.

When the men and their dogs are done, the Scouts stand and cheer and then, of course, it's a which-Cub-Scout-can-cheer-loudest contest. Before Navy has a chance to make a case for staying longer, and before I get stuck talking to Elsie Jenkins again, I grab my brother by the arm and lead him out of the building.

We talk about those dogs the whole walk home.

CHAPTER THREE

My parents say my life doesn't really revolve around my little brother's, but it sure seems that way. Tuesday afternoons I pick up Navy and take him around the block from our house to his friend Cullen's house. Cullen's father is their soccer coach and drives them to practice. Usually, I go home afterward and play with Maybe and get my homework done. But today there's something I really want to do, so I ask Cullen's dad if he has room in his car for me too. Because what I want to do is hang with JennaLouiseNoSpace, who lives two blocks from the soccer field. (If you're wondering about her name, that's how JennaLouise always introduces herself.)

Life can be so random. It's possible that JennaLouise and I might not have become best friends if it hadn't been for the Fisher-Price doll family at Little Ones Nursery School. There was this girl, Gabrielle, who was determined to destroy them. She held them underwater in the sand-and-water table. She laid them on the alphabet carpet and built crushing block towers over their small plastic bodies. She stomped on them.

How could I let her do that? I took those dolls, and Miss Catherine and Miss Holly could not pry them away from me. Sharing was an important part of daily life at Little Ones, so my behavior landed me on the red Thinking Bench day after day. I also would not stop calling Gabrielle *Grabrielle,* at least in whispered secrets to JennaLouise.

JennaLouise sat right next to me, our little three-year-old hips touching, during my time-outs. She hadn't done anything wrong, or anything that she needed to *think about*, to use Little Ones language. She barely knew me, but for some reason I had a new friend sitting faithfully by my side each day I ended up on the bench.

Finally, a teacher put the dolls away, never to be seen again. I missed them, but at least I knew they were safe from Grabrielle.

And the friendship of my life was born. There's always been a basic, no-words-needed understanding between us. A feeling of something a lot like comfort that I've never felt with anyone else.

When I get to JennaLouise's house, her sister, Margaret Ann (with a space), is in the kitchen making cupcakes and frosting from scratch for a bake sale at the high school.

Their mom, Daphne, is in getting-out-of-the-house mode, racing around and looking at lists and wondering where her keys are even though they're in her hand. I think she's actually organized most of the time—she works as a fundraiser/event and party planner, so she kind of has to be—but even I know that when Daphne has to leave the house at a certain time, she is more like a tornado than a mom.

"I have fifteen minutes before I'm supposed to meet the client and it's twenty-five minutes away."

"Not ideal," Margaret Ann says.

"Not helpful," Daphne says back, but it's all with smiles.

"Go," Margaret Ann says. "Stop talking."

Daphne kisses the top of Margaret Ann's head, Jenna-Louise's, then mine, and it's not weird—just nice. Like everything here.

The house itself seems to sigh after she leaves. Margaret Ann gets back to frosting while JennaLouise and I sit at the counter and watch.

The vintage flowered apron Margaret Ann's wearing makes her look like an ad for something I could never afford or even figure out how to wear. But curses are flying as she tries to even out the milk chocolate frosting on a plateful of cupcakes. She messes up two beyond repair, which is the exact right number of mistakes for JennaLouise and me.

JennaLouise eats hers from the bottom up. "Ross ting zest," she says with a very full mouth, which I think means *frosting's best.* I cut the cake part of the cupcake in half and place one piece on top of the frosting—a frosting sandwich. Together we sing Margaret Ann's praises for the deliciousness, still praise-singing as JennaLouise pours big glasses of milk, which we gulp down.

"Thank you so much," I say. "I just ate the most delicious thing I ever ate, so it's a pretty big day in my life."

Margaret Ann says, "I'll send you a card on this date next year to mark the occasion. October ninth. Got it."

"Don't bother with the card," I say. "Just bake more cupcakes."

"I'll be in college then," she says, and that makes us all go still. It's not like we don't know she's a senior, but it's the first time the thought of her not being around feels real. Ugh. It feels like everyone's leaving—the Rooneys, and in less than a year, Margaret Ann too.

"It's not magic, you know," Margaret Ann says.

"You mean there are applications and all that? I know. I never thought—"

JennaLouise laughs. "She meant the cupcakes." And I guess that was obvious to her—there are things sisters get about each other. And these two are *such* sisters. Like on the first day of school, the teacher always asks JennaLouise if she's Margaret Ann's sister. JennaLouise pretends to act annoyed but I know she's actually proud. They're both tall, with the perfect kind of straight brown hair. The tall comes from their dad, Dennis, who's almost never home because he owns three car dealerships.

JennaLouise and Margaret Ann are both so beautiful you might even hate them a little if they weren't so nice.

I know nothing about that kind of sibling relationship. Navy is a ginger (a rare thing; it's from Dad's side of the family) and already almost as tall as me. I'm short. Not ginger, just plain old brown hair, brown eyes. Not anything you'd notice, really.

They're both staring at me. Right. Cupcakes. "My mom doesn't bake," I say, and that should win me an award for understatement. Or kindness. Or something. My mom is a terrible cook and my dad doesn't cook at all. When I've needed a baked-something to bring to school, it's always been store-bought. Which is fine. ShopHereNow has fantastic cupcakes. I'm not deprived.

"I have something astonishing to tell you," Margaret Ann says. "You don't need your mommy to do this for you. *You* can bake."

Wow. It honestly never occurred to me I could do this by myself.

"Want me to send you the recipe?" Margaret Ann asks.

I'm nodding, excited, and I catch a glimpse of JennaLouise, who is sighing and reaching for her backpack. "I'm going to get started on homework," she says, "while you hijack my best friend. Are you going to share your secret ingredient?"

Margaret Ann tilts her head, like she's thinking about it.

"It's extra cocoa," JennaLouise says. "Twice as much as the recipe says."

"Your secret's safe with me," I say.

CHAPTER FOUR

At dinner that night, Mom asks, for the third time, if I'm sure I don't want some black beans.

I nod yes. Couldn't be surer. Mom moves the serving spoon, loaded with beans, in my direction anyway. I hold up my hand. No. No beans.

Navy holds up his hand too. Beans: not a big hit at the Morand family dinner table.

Mom bangs the metal bean bowl back down. She's been a little cranky lately.

My parents are in the disaster business. Their company, Never Happened, does repairs to homes and businesses after floods, fires, and storms, and lately there haven't been a ton of disasters.

"Army, why aren't you eating?"

"Because I've never liked beans and never eat them." Every time a bean accidentally enters my mouth—usually by hiding under delicious chips and cheese on a nacho platter—ew.

But now I feel bad. Not bad enough to eat beans, but bad.

There's old-looking salad on the table and bread. I tear

off a big piece. I think about the cupcake I had earlier and look at my phone to check the recipe.

"Put that away," Mom says. "You know the rules."

"I do," I say. "But do we have flour, sugar, cocoa, vanilla, those kinds of things?"

"Why would we?" Mom asks.

I think of what's in the cabinets. She's right. "Could you get some? I want to try to make these cupcakes Margaret Ann baked today."

"Why?" Mom asks.

"Because they're delicious? Because it's nice to sometimes eat something that's delicious." Oops. That came out sounding nastier than I meant.

Mom gives me a look. It is not filled with love. "I'm going to the grocery store right after dinner, so write down what you want."

I stand and walk to the pad of paper Mom keeps next to the refrigerator.

"You don't need to do it now," she says.

I look at the recipe Margaret Ann sent me again and write everything down. "It's done," I say.

"Armed Forces," Dad says to Navy and me. "When dinner's done, please clean up and sweep the kitchen floor."

I swear, they named my brother Navy just so they could say that Armed Forces thing. They think it's hilarious.

The name I was actually given on the day I was born was Mary. Not the most original name, but not the kind that makes substitute teachers call your name for attendance like it's a mistake that will soon be corrected: *Leah? Zeke? Marcus? Ar-meeee?!?!*

Someone with confused fingers at a florist shop near the hospital made a mistake on the card that came with flowers Aunt Emily sent when I was born. It said: *Congratulations on the birth of your beautiful new daughter, Army.*

Just a mistake. A scrambling of letters. An anagram.

My parents, as a joke, called me Army for the first few days of my life. Then it stuck. Ha ha ha. Mom said it felt destined to be. And yes, they made the change before my birth certificate was created, so it's official.

But it's just my name now. I can't imagine having a different one.

Navy sighs about the cleanup and sweeping. Which is what I was about to do, but luckily he did it, so this time he's the one Mom glares at.

"You mean, 'Of course, Dad. We always want to help out our family'?" Mom says.

"Yes," Navy says. "And I also want to say I'm in favor of cupcakes." That might be the most support he has ever shown for me, and yes, I am aware that it has nothing to do with me, but I still smile at him.

"I'm going to hose down the truck while it's still light out," Dad says. "The Armed Forces can hold down the fort."

Navy starts fake laughing and pretends to fall off his chair. Morand family fact: you cannot say anything within a letter or two of the word *fart* in front of Navy without getting this reaction.

When Navy gets tired of being ignored and climbs back on his chair, he looks around and asks, " 'Scused?" He is out of his chair before anyone can answer. His plate clatters into the sink and then his footsteps clomp clomp clomp up the stairs.

"Isn't he supposed to help clean up?" I ask.

"If you clean up, that means he'll have to sweep," Mom says, like she's offering me something great I can't refuse. A floor after it's been swept by Navy looks exactly the same as it looked before, but that's not really my problem. I move Navy's plate from the sink into the dishwasher. Mom usually saves anything left over, but I make the decision to throw away those nasty beans. "You can wrap the rest of that salad and bring it for lunch tomorrow, Army."

"Okay," I say, but I know I will "forget" it at home. When a salad is not good the day it's made, it is not better the next day.

Mom and Dad leave and once I finish wiping down the counters, I reach for Maybe's bowls and food. He eats the same food every morning and night, and it makes him so happy! His mouth is open in a big smile, his tail wagging even though he's sitting.

After he eats, he follows me until I put my sneakers on and leash him up and head outside. I wave at Dad, but I don't think he sees me.

There's a lawn mower going somewhere but at least it's not nearby. I wish I lived in a quieter time before lawn mowers and leaf blowers, when people just used rakes, or possibly oxen.

I hear the sound of a car behind me, so I hop up onto the sidewalk, and Maybe hops up too. Johnny on the Spot—everyone calls him that, though I have no idea why—is prowling in his old truck, looking at the junk people brought to the curb for bulk trash pickup tomorrow. He lives in our neighborhood and I've seen him hauling away lawn chairs, barbecue grills, skis and sleds, half a motorcycle, metal filing cabinets. My parents sometimes hire him to haul stuff away when they don't need a whole dumpster on-site at a job.

Even though I'm still a little hungry, I'm starting to feel the best kind of filled up—just soaking in the joy Maybe gets from everything—the smell of the fire hydrant on the corner, squirrels chasing circles around the Sandersons' oak tree, the bush he likes to pee on.

I'm about to turn and walk back home when something catches my eye.

What's in that tree? I bring Maybe into the street for a better look. There are dangling legs, a flash of green. It's a little kid, moving steadily, boldly, practically walking up the branches of the tree in the Hunts' front yard across the street. There's no hesitation, no thinking about the next move. Hand reaches, foot follows. No looking down, just up, up, up, branch to branch, reaching out with hands at the right time.

Maybe pulls me toward the front door. I bring him

inside, take off his leash, freshen his water. And then I think about that kid in the tree. Maybe the Hunts have visitors?

I go back outside. Nothing.

There's no way I just imagined a little kid racing up a tree.

Is there?

CHAPTER FIVE

Through some amazing miracle involving Cullen's father picking the boys up after school for a soccer scrimmage game and my parents meeting a client about a possible job, Jenna-Louise and I have Wednesday afternoon to ourselves.

"Where's good food?" she asks after her mom drops her off. We walk into the kitchen, where she plops herself down in Dad's seat.

"Wrong house for good food," I say, though she already knows it. I open the refrigerator, hoping that inside I'll find some other family's food. But no. I take out juice Mom made with old vegetables and fruit. "Try not to look at it. Be sure not to notice it's brown."

JennaLouise is brave. She takes a sip. "It's not too bad." I think of the food I eat at her house—the most delicious cupcakes and cookies and brownies—and feel, not for the first time, that it's kind of pathetic that "not too bad" is the best the Morand family can do. Especially when it's not even true. The juice is pretty bad.

But then I remember the groceries I put away yesterday.

"Do you feel like baking? We could make Margaret Ann's chocolate cupcakes. I have the recipe."

"And the secret ingredient?"

"Yeah, we got it all."

"I guess," she says. "We did just have cupcakes yesterday."

"And your point is?" I take out all the ingredients. I text my mom so she can't say I baked without first checking with her about turning on the oven or something, which is exactly the kind of thing she would say even though she thinks it's perfectly fine for me to be in charge of the oven when she's out and needs me to stick some practically inedible thing in there for dinner.

I'm glad JennaLouise is here for a lot of reasons, but especially for the sake of these cupcakes. Apparently dry ingredients have to be separate from wet ingredients until a certain point when they can meet. I worry sometimes that there are whole chunks of knowledge, specific things like that, that no one has ever bothered to tell me.

We add the extra cocoa and then a little more and through some miracle (it's a day of miracles!) I remember that the cupcake pan is downstairs, mixed in with all the Never Happened supplies and other kitchen equipment rarely used, like a pasta machine Aunt Emily gave my parents for Christmas. Our basement is gross, so I tell JennaLouise to wait in the kitchen.

So gross. My parents, my mother especially, are orderly.

More than orderly. Sort of military about order. Except for the basement. It's stacked with everything Never Happened uses on a regular basis—wet/dry vacs, an extra generator that only sometimes works, buckets, ladders. It smells awful and it's hard to move because everything is packed in. But my parents are ridiculously proud of the fact that our basement never floods, and that's why they stash *everything* there. Well, not quite everything. They have so much stuff there's some in the garage and in a storage space they rent.

I spot old pots and pans on top of the metal shelving, and teetering on top of them, the cupcake pan. Covered with cobwebs. Ew!

I go upstairs and bring it outside to shake it out, then wash it in the kitchen sink. Twice. That's the kind of gross it is.

We line the pan with paper liners—I didn't remember to put that on the list, but somehow Mom got them anyway—and we fill the cupcake pan with the batter and put it in the oven.

I run upstairs to get my Language Arts book so Jenna-Louise and I can get some homework done. Maybe is right next to me, never letting me out of his sight. As I'm coming downstairs, I am greeted by a smell. Mostly chocolate but maybe also butter? It is the best smell ever smelled in our house!

"Do you still refuse to put clothes on Maybe?" Jenna-Louise asks.

"Of course," I say. Dignity.

"Because I saw this dog koala costume for Halloween, and it was basically made for Maybe. You could just try it."

"No," I say. Maybe makes the sound, like a sigh, that he sometimes makes when he's finished turning circles before settling in for sleep.

I load all the bowls and spatulas into the dishwasher and instead of getting started on homework, I ask, "Should we make the frosting now?"

"The cupcakes will still have to cool when they come out," she says.

"Right," I say.

We get through four vocabulary words before the timer goes off and I open the oven door.

I place the cupcake pan on the stove and just stand there, breathing. I want to live with this smell for the rest of my life.

I spread a dish towel on the counter and carefully pluck all the cupcakes out of the tin. Then I remember that the mudroom, where our washing machine is, is always the coolest part of the house, so I move them onto the bench in there. The sooner they're cool, the sooner we can frost them. And we can eat them. They smell *fantastic.*

JennaLouise and I go to my room to get through the rest of our homework before making the frosting. But we end up watching some videos on her phone before we start the vocab. Once we're done, we go back downstairs. I'm about to get the butter and confectioners' sugar when JennaLouise gets a text from her mom. She groans. "I have to go."

"No way," I say. "We have to frost these. And eat them."

"I know. My mom needs me to help her with something—she didn't know she was supposed to wrap the party favors for some event so—"

"Can't she wrap them?" I ask.

"It's more than three hundred favors and the event is tomorrow. Do you want to help?"

I nod. Why does that sound like so much fun? "Let me just check with my mom."

"Let me check first," she says. She sends a text to her mom and starts packing up her backpack. Her phone beeps and she says, "If you stay for dinner, it's pizza and Mom says you can choose the toppings as thanks for helping."

I text my mom, and she agrees, and we go downstairs to wait until Margaret Ann pulls in the driveway in her car to take us to a land where instead of floods and fires, it's all about wrapping presents and celebrations.

CHAPTER SIX

Though I have never done anything like this before, I seem to have a gift for wrapping tiny little jars with fairy lights inside them in cellophane. I get three wrapped for every one JennaLouise and her mom each do.

"It's a strangely specific skill set you have yourself there, Army," Daphne says. "But I, for one, am very grateful."

The jars look so beautiful when the lights are turned on. JennaLouise keeps arranging them in bunches of three—which look beautiful together. And then in fives and sevens, which also look beautiful together. She claims this will help her mother know how to arrange them at whatever fundraiser this is for. Her mother tells her to cut it out and start packing the wrapped jars into boxes so she can load them in her car for tomorrow.

JennaLouise, while not a great wrapper, is a fast boxer-upper, so we finish pretty quickly.

And eat great pizza.

And regret that we forgot to bring the cupcakes along, because they would have been a fine dessert. But of course, this being JennaLouise's house, dessert is not an issue. There are three kinds of Ben & Jerry's in the freezer.

I want to sleep over, but school nights have always been out of the question, so I don't even bother asking.

I get home at eight and find Mom in the kitchen.

Wait.

Where's Maybe?

"Mom? Have you seen Maybe?"

"Ah, yes," she says, turning to look at me. "It has apparently been a day of dietary indiscretions." That's what the vet calls it when Maybe eats something he isn't supposed to.

"Ew," I say. "Sorry."

"I put him in the yard three times—he kept asking to go out, and I did have the pleasure of cleaning up a pile of vomit," she says.

"MAYBE!!!!" I call. I look in the living room. Not there. On the landing of the stairs. Not there.

I run into my room and Maybe's there. Not in his bed. On the floor next to it. I can tell he doesn't feel well before I even smell him—seriously, his body gives off this weird smell when his stomach's upset. The first two times it happened, we rushed him to the vet. And learned that we don't need to do that (Mom made that clear the second time she paid the vet bill). It's full-on gross, but Maybe eats stuff and then . . . other things happen that eventually make him feel better. For example, I once learned that he had eaten one of

Navy's socks when I took him for a walk. That was not pleasant. (Are you getting this? He pooped out the sock.)

"Hey, buddy," I say. He lifts his head the very tiniest bit and I scratch his neck and then his ears. "I'm sorry," I say. "Being sick is the worst. You'll feel better in the morning."

I wake to the realization that Maybe is *not* staring at me.

He's at the door to my room, on his side. He tries to stand but takes a step and lies down again. He keeps lying down with a soft, sad moan, and then standing to move to another spot. And he's panting. Hard. More than he ever pants. "Maybe!" I yell, racing over. His body's too warm. It's more than my heart can stand. "MOM! MOM!"

I hear her steps and then she's at my door.

"Maybe's really sick," I say.

She walks into the room. "You know how he is when he eats something he's not supposed to eat."

"But what did he eat?! He's never been sick like this!"

Mom shrugs.

"And usually he throws up and feels better," I say, panic rising. "You said he threw up last night, but he obviously isn't better and I've never seen him panting like this and he can't get comfortable and we need to bring him to the vet."

Mom shrugs again. "I don't think they'd be open—oh, they do have early hours one day—I could call and see."

"Mom! We need to move. Like now."

I put on my sneakers and wrap Maybe in a blanket from

my bed. "Let's just go," I say, "and if they're closed we'll find an animal hospital or something."

She expects to argue with me, but I'm holding Maybe close and running downstairs and heading outside to wait in the car. I don't know what to do. My mother obviously doesn't know what to do. Dr. Jenkins will know what to do.

Eventually, Mom gets in and we drive to the vet's office. Dr. Jenkins is outside and turning to unlock the door. I bolt from the car with Maybe in my arms.

"He's really sick," I say. "Can you please, can you—"

Mom catches up to me. "Army, give Dr. Jenkins some time to get settled. We can wait."

"Let's see what's happening here," Dr. Jenkins says, leading us into the waiting room. She motions for us to follow her as she flips on the lights and takes us into an exam room.

She takes Maybe from my arms just as Mom's cell rings. I'm annoyed when she answers. Why can't she just be here, with me, helping Maybe?

"Wait, what?" she says into the phone. "How many?"

Is she seriously dealing with work stuff now?

She looks at me. "Did you make the cupcakes?" she asks.

Why does that matter? I can't even form words.

"Dad found wrappers in the mudroom. I think Maybe's just sick because he ate... it sounds like seven of your cupcakes."

I guess I'd feel sick if I ate seven cupcakes.

"Were they chocolate?" Dr. Jenkins asks.

Dogs and chocolate.

Dogs can't eat chocolate.

I am nearly certain dogs can die if they eat chocolate.

I burst into tears.

"Let me take a look," Dr. Jenkins says, putting him on the table. I want to pick him up and hold him against me and tell him I'm sorry. I was careless and I am so sorry.

"Do you remember the kind of chocolate, or how much you used?"

"Two kinds," I say. "That unsweetened chocolate and also a lot of cocoa."

She makes a face, like a grimace or something. Like that's bad news. And my heart is racing and I cannot live through this. I can't.

"How long ago do you think he ate it?" She puts her stethoscope on Maybe's chest and listens.

I sit down, right on the exam room floor, because my legs can't hold me anymore. "I wasn't home," I say. "I don't know. Could have been yesterday around dinnertime?"

"I found vomit when I came home at six," Mom says.

"Okay," Dr. Jenkins says. "There is cause for concern. Maybe's very small and we don't know how much chocolate he consumed. He's going to need to stay here today. I'll hook him to an IV and see what we can do."

I can't go home without Maybe. "Can I stay with him?"

My mother puts up her hand, as though Dr. Jenkins doesn't have to answer that. "Of course not, Army. Dr. Jenkins will take care of him."

I can't. I can't leave him here in a cage, attached to tubes, wondering why he's here and where I am. Dr. Jenkins lifts Maybe up and says, "We'll take good care of him." She walks through a door at the back of the exam room.

"Let's go, Army," Mom says. "I'll drop you at—you're in pajamas. You're still in your pajamas?"

"I can't," I say. And it means everything. I can't be in my pajamas. I can't leave Maybe here. I can't have done what I did. And I can't be dropped off anywhere. I need to be here with him.

CHAPTER SEVEN

My body changes out of pajamas, makes lunch, and goes to school. It moves from class to class. It sits with JennaLouise at lunch but cannot tell her. It sneaks into the bathroom to text Mom for an update, but she doesn't have one and also tells me to stop texting from school, like it's just a normal day and I'm asking what's for dinner.

When I get off the bus and am walking to the house, Mom is waiting on the front steps. My brain is not able to figure out what that means until she reaches out her arms to me and says, "Army, I am so sorry."

"What?" I say. There are lots of bad things that aren't the worst thing. Maybe might have to stay overnight. Or need surgery or something. Not everything is the worst thing.

"Maybe died, honey, I'm so sorry," she says. "Dr. Jenkins said it was just too much for a dog so little, she did everything that she could do but she couldn't save him."

"Wait, you—he's—he isn't—? What?"

"He died, and I'm so, so sorry."

I think I scream—I open my mouth and a sound comes

out—but I also feel like I'm in another world, a world that is awful, one in which I cannot keep standing there with my mother telling me that Maybe is no longer alive. I run up to my room and close the door and lie on my bed. I look at Maybe's bed. And that wasn't a great idea, because I try to imagine a life without him and I don't want to. I don't want that. And the tears come.

I wish my crying was loud enough to drown out everything but unfortunately, I hear Navy, some combination of yelling and crying, and it's awful, because I can't even hold my own hurt, and there's all this other hurt too.

Through the afternoon there are knocks at my door, my mother and then my father. I'm almost tempted to let Dad in. He's the one who usually gets how I'm feeling, but I can't.

I cannot. I cannot live in this world that doesn't have Maybe in it. I cry until I'm sick from crying but can't stop and eventually, at some point, I fall asleep.

CHAPTER EIGHT

It is cruel. I wake up. And there's a blip of time, a fraction of a second, before I remember and then I'm hit so hard with this new fact. What makes it even crueler is that there's no one looking at me, waiting for me to wake. No one stamping his tiny little Muppet paws with impatience. Maybe's bed is empty. Maybe's bed will always be empty.

I pull the covers over my head and the tears start before I even form a single idea in my head about how I can survive in this new life. This life in which not only did my sweet dog die but it was entirely my fault.

There's a loud knock on the door and my mother says, "You can't miss the bus today," which aren't exactly the sympathetic words a person might expect to hear on a morning like this, but my mother likes routine.

I pull on clothes from a pile on my dresser—not even sure if it's dirty laundry for me to wash or clean clothes to be folded and put away. Who can remember? That was a whole other life. And now . . . ugh, I keep looking at the bed. Maybe's empty bed.

I walk down the stairs with only five minutes left until I have to leave to catch the bus. Navy's eating his breakfast and avoiding my eyes. But I can see that his are red, just like his nose. I'm glad I didn't look in any mirrors this morning—I don't want to see what I look like.

I wonder if Navy knows it was my fault.

I keep thinking I see Maybe, hear the jingle of his tags. I almost feel his presence. You know how some people who've lost a leg say they can still feel their leg? A phantom limb. I'm feeling my phantom Maybe following me, reminding me to take our morning walk around the block. To feed him before I go to school. To hug all my love into him before I leave.

And then, like a blow to the side of my head, I look down in the corner where Maybe's food and water bowls are, but they're gone.

The leash is no longer hanging on a hook by the mudroom door.

The small basket of tennis balls and toys he liked to play with—gone.

All the signs of his life are gone.

Never happened.

I can only go through the motions, can't think, so I'm amazed that I have the idea to go into the storage closet in the mudroom and grab a whole box of tissues to squish down into my backpack. I wish I had a note for my teachers, something saying *Please don't expect Army to act like a functioning human today because she is not. She is barely human and not at all functioning. If possible, do not look her in the eye. Thank you.*

JennaLouise. I didn't tell her and I cannot face her. She will take one look at me and know. I could just text her and get it over with, but then it'll exist, as a text, this awful thing, this horrible fact, and I know I can delete it, but what if she doesn't? Or what if it lives forever in a cloud? I don't know why, but as soon as I get on the bus, I pull out my spiral Science notebook, tear out a page, and write the worst words that exist—*Maybe died.* I fold it up, but I need to write more: *I cannot talk about it or about him or about anything. Probably forever. Please don't ask anything and could you just talk the whole time at lunch because I cannot talk. Thank you, I love you.*

"A note?" JennaLouise says at her locker. I nod.

I try to walk away, but JennaLouise reads the note and comes after me. She's about to hug me, but it's like she sees the crying I'm trying not to do and so she just reaches out and squeezes my hand. "I have plenty to tell you at lunch. I will talk so much you might wish you never asked me to."

I would smile if I were me, but I don't know what I am. Just that I'm not me.

I am a body that goes from class to class. Or at least that's what I mean to do, but I get stuck in the hall outside Language Arts second period. My legs refuse to move me into the classroom. Ms. Davenport spots me and comes out into the hall. She looks down, like she wants me to look into her eyes, but I can't. "Are you okay?" she asks. I shake my head. I'm standing there, trying to figure out how not to burst into tears when JennaLouise appears, takes one look at the situation, and says, "Hey, Ms. Davenport. Can I talk to you for a second?"

I stand there, stuck, until JennaLouise gives me a friendly shove into the classroom.

I guess I didn't need that note for my teachers, because either they can tell not to call on me or JennaLouise talks to them all before I get to their class.

Every period, I try to make it until the halfway-through point before I grab the hall pass and make a run for the bathroom, where I sit in a stall. Try to take deep breaths. Try not to cry. Cry. Flush the toilet in case anyone is in there, because ew, who wants to be the girl who doesn't flush? Splash cold water on my face, try to dry it with school-bathroom paper towels, which have never absorbed anything.

Most days, I can't wait for lunch. But today I just want to be home, but no, that's the last place I want to be. There's no place to be. I sit with JennaLouise at our table and realize I forgot to pack something to eat. It doesn't matter—I wouldn't be able to eat anyway.

I look around, making sure no one is staring at me—I feel like an obvious mess, an unraveling person. Everything's as it always is. People sit where they sit, talk to who they talk to; it never changes. I would never plop my tray down at Leah and Marley's table or the girls' soccer team's or any table other than the one where JennaLouise and I always sit.

But that's exactly what Elsie Jenkins does. Without even a *Hey, is this seat taken?* or a *Do you guys mind if*... she blows in like a storm, slams her backpack down, sticks up her index finger to indicate she'll be back, then heads to the food line.

"Have you and Elsie Jenkins been hanging out or something?" JennaLouise asks in a voice that makes it clear she knows we have not.

I'm trying to muster up the ability to talk, to tell JennaLouise I saw Elsie Jenkins at Navy's school, but JennaLouise says, "Never mind. I forgot. You don't have to talk. I'll talk. Do you want some of my lunch? I have that good turkey from the place you like."

I shake my head. I don't want to eat or talk or do any of the mouth things.

Elsie Jenkins comes back with a tray of food and a stack of napkins. "I'm a really sloppy eater," she says. She sits next to JennaLouise, and stares at me. "Were you guys in the middle of something, because—"

"Actually," JennaLouise says, "today's kind of a weird day, so if there's some other time—"

Elsie Jenkins doesn't listen. "Because, Army, I was thinking we should get the PTA to book a visit from that group. Service with a Wag."

What is she even talking about? Oh, those dogs. I don't want to think about dogs. Why can't Elsie Jenkins talk to me when we're in Language Arts instead of when JennaLouise is going to talk all the way through lunch so I don't have to think or talk?

"Army and I saw this amazing presentation about service dogs—did she tell you about it?"

"No," JennaLouise says.

"Actually, there's a lot of planning that goes into approaching the PTA. They have very specific things you need to do. There's a request form we have to get from the main office and fill out about why it would be 'educationally significant' and we need to get student signatures on a petition. So Army, I was thinking you could come over one day and we could fill out the form after school at my house but if you'd rather do it now, that works too." When she finally stops talking, she shovels a very overfull spork of mashed potatoes into her mouth.

"She'll come over," JennaLouise says. Right before I kick her under the table. I totally get that JennaLouise, in that moment, would do anything, including throwing her own miserable, silent, can't-talk-or-she'll-cry best friend to the wolves, just to get Elsie Jenkins to stop talking. It's almost like she's rescuing me. Except for the way she just promised Elsie Jenkins I'd go to her house. Which is the opposite of a rescue.

Elsie Jenkins says, "Oh, okay. Cool." I think that she's going to pick up her tray now and head back to wherever she usually sits. But instead she turns to JennaLouise and asks, "Do you want to come too?"

JennaLouise, whose mouth is full, shakes her head no.

At the end of lunch, Elsie Jenkins says, "Let me know what day next week works and have your mom send a note so you can come home on my bus."

I stare at Elsie Jenkins at the very same instant I am kicking JennaLouise under the table again. Hard. But at least I'm not crying at school.

I somehow survive the whole day without bursting into tears where anyone can see me. A miracle. But who cares—the only miracle I want can't really happen. The foreverness of this . . . I just can't.

CHAPTER NINE

I ride the bus like the zombie I am and get off a stop early, near Mr. Hoffart's house. Today, at least, I have to see if Mr. Hoffart's paper's still there, at the top of his driveway. It isn't. I hope he didn't hurt himself walking up and down that long driveway to get it.

The lightest drizzle mists the air but that doesn't make me move faster. I'm in no hurry to get home. Home, where it happened. Home, where my mother cleaned up all evidence that Maybe ever existed. Wait.

What is that?

Or who is that?

I walk faster, hurrying to get closer to . . . whatever that is.

It's a little girl.

Right in the middle of the street.

Barefoot.

The girl is walking in the same direction as I am down my street, Marigold Street, but slower, so I gain on her without having to run.

She's wearing a white dress, or maybe it's a nightgown,

with pink and red roses. She walks slowly. A blond ponytail hangs down her back. I think it's the same kid who was climbing that tree!

I call out, "Hey, excuse me. Do you need some help? Are you lost?"

The girl doesn't look at me. She doesn't slow down.

How does it make any sense for a little girl to be in the middle of the street all by herself? Why isn't she wearing shoes? Where are her parents?

"Hi," I say, walking sideways alongside her. "We should go on the sidewalk. Do you need some help?" She's younger than Navy, maybe six or seven? Why isn't she listening to me?

Maybe she can't hear. I want to touch her shoulder but can almost feel something sparking in the air, telling me not to touch this girl, to just keep an eye on her. To keep this all-by-herself child safe. To do a better job of keeping someone safe.

The girl turns suddenly, steps onto the sidewalk, tiptoes down the Rooneys' driveway to their house, slips between two big bushes, and opens a window. She lifts a knee up onto the low ledge, swings her body around, and closes the window, disappearing inside.

I run toward my house. "Mom! Mom!" I burst through the front door and race straight to the kitchen table, where Mom's reading something written on a pad.

She puts up a finger, the thing she does when she doesn't want to be interrupted.

"No. Mom. Listen. There's this girl. I don't know her, but she was outside and barefoot, just walking in the middle of the street and then she went into the Rooneys' old house but through the window."

"Whose?" Mom asks, her voice steady—one of the perks of a mom trained in dealing with disasters. She slides her feet into shoes by the front door and follows me outside as I try to explain.

"The Rooneys' place, I guess the people who moved in? Have you met them?"

Mom shakes her head. "Let's be careful here. We need to tell the parents, but we will not be sticking our noses in their business." According to my parents, that's just about the worst thing you can do.

As we're walking, she pauses and asks, "How are you doing?" like she just remembered about Maybe. I can't even imagine a time when it won't be the main thing, the saddest thing, at the center of my brain.

I shake my head, because I know she won't want to hear the true answer. Also it kind of means not so good. But Mom and I don't really talk about feelings and anyway there's no time now as we cross the street and head up the Rooneys' walkway.

Mom rings the bell and we wait. The door slowly opens and a woman holding a baby is standing there, giving us a puzzled look. There's a glob of white spit-up on her shoulder and it looks like she might have forgotten to brush her hair today.

I wait for Mom to start talking but she is just standing there, so I start. "Hi. I'm Army Morand. I live right over there." I turn and point to my house. "I know it's weird to ring your doorbell when you don't know me and also, hi? Welcome to the neighborhood, but I wanted to tell you that I saw a girl—do you have a daughter?"

"Madison?" she says.

"Is Madison a blond little girl? I saw her walking down the street—she was in the street—and she was barefoot . . ."

The woman nods but looks otherwise frozen.

"She's home now," I say. ". . . came in the window?" I'm not sure why that comes out as a question, because she definitely did go in the window. "And I'm pretty sure I saw her another time, climbing a tree." I wait for the woman to explain but all there is is silence.

Finally, my mother speaks up. I am so relieved she's going to take over until she says, "I forgot the basket. I'll be right back."

Whenever someone new moves to the neighborhood, Mom brings a basket packed with stuff—menus for local restaurants, some food, information about Never Happened. And apparently it couldn't wait another minute, because she's off, leaving me in the company of the new neighbor who doesn't seem to know how conversations go—first one person talks, then the other. Repeat.

The woman watches my mother head to our house, then says, "Thank you. Really, thank you so much for letting me know." From inside the house I hear a baby—another baby—cry. The woman is about to close the door, but then she looks at me again. "What did you say your name was?"

"Army. And that was my mom, Michelle. She's very serious about new-neighbor basket deliveries."

"Well, that's sweet. I need to go check on . . ." Her voice trails off as she looks behind her. And she seems to almost come awake, and realize what happened, and that I'm standing there, because she shakes her head and says, quietly, "What you must think."

I shrug like I don't think anything at all, because I can't exactly blurt, *Why was your kid out in the middle of the street?* Then I say, "I'll tell my mom to leave the basket on your stoop."

"Okay. So long, Army. Someday you're going to have to tell me how you got that awesome name," she says as she closes the door.

Right. Awesome. Like it wasn't all just a big mistake.

I start walking home, very slowly. I am in no rush to be in our Maybeless house.

CHAPTER TEN

I go right up to my room and close the door. It's Friday, at least, so I don't have to worry about my brain not being able to do homework—I can just be in my room.

Shoot. Where's Maybe's bed? Never happened.

I am probably going to be crying for the rest of my life. I can't imagine it ever changing. I can't. I killed my dog. Who is so careless that she leaves chocolate where a dog can get it? Who doesn't notice how sick her dog is that night—what if we had taken him to the hospital then? Would he still be alive? I can't bear to think of that. I can't bear to think of anything.

I crawl into bed and pull the blankets over me. Then I cry and cry and at some point I must fall asleep, because I wake to knocking. "It's time for dinner," Mom says.

Mom doesn't seem to care that I don't respond. She knocks again. "Come on, Army. Let's go."

When I don't answer, she opens the door. I can't see it with blankets piled up on top of me, but I know the sound. The mattress sinks as she sits down near my feet.

She touches my leg. "Army, this will get easier. Eventually, time will erase the pain."

That sounds not only untrue, but not even like what I want. I know my parents' job is to erase the hard things that happen to people, or really, to their houses, but Mom never understood Maybe. She didn't have pets growing up. We only got him because Dad and I wore her down. I don't want to have lost Maybe. And I definitely don't want to forget him.

"You need to eat dinner. I let you stay up here last night, but tonight I'm going to insist."

Right. Because I should be all better in a day.

She pulls the covers down and stares into my face. "You need to come downstairs now."

I slide into my chair and when my eyes fall on Navy, it's like he's measuring me, wondering if I'll break or blow away. His eyes are still red too.

I know not to look at Dad because the love in his eyes will make me lose it. "Hey, Army," Dad says, his voice soft and careful. He squeezes my left shoulder and keeps his hand there for a noticeably long time.

Each time Dad passes a serving plate to me—salad, chicken, rice—I pass it on to Navy. Mom and Dad are ignoring the way Navy is slobbering his food up and chewing with his mouth wide open. And that I have no food on my plate. And haven't said a word. They're just talking about this big storm that hit Georgia and how they're upset it didn't hit

New Jersey. They don't want anyone to get hurt, of course, but storms are good for business.

It's not the first time I've thought this, but it is the first time I ask out loud: "Does it depress you?"

"Does what depress me?" Mom asks, squinting.

"Never Happened. Always dealing with people who are getting through some kind of disaster."

"It does the opposite of depress me!" Mom nearly yells. She picks up her napkin and wipes it hard across her mouth. "What kind of question is that?!"

I reach for the salad tongs, pick out two slices of cucumber, and put them on my plate. "An honest one."

Dad puts his fork down. "Your mother and I help people. I don't see what could be depressing about that." He doesn't sound defensive like Mom. Just puzzled.

What they're saying makes sense but doesn't answer this other part that's been gnawing at me. "The way you have to tell people over and over that 'they're only things, they still have their memories.' And also that you only make money if someone's life gets wrecked."

They're looking at me, both of them, like I've just suggested that we, from this point forward, commit our lives to cannibalism. Like I'm the strangest being they've ever encountered.

"You're forgetting about the hurricane boxes," Dad says. "We don't only mop up afterward."

Their hurricane boxes are filled with supplies that help people get through storms and power outages.

"Not that there's any shame in mopping up afterward," Mom says. "It's necessary work. I'm proud to do it."

It's true. She didn't even wait a whole day to clear away Maybe's bowls. I can't keep myself from looking where they used to be. And of course I'm crying. Again.

"Army." Mom's voice is soft and I know she is going to S P E A K   V E R Y   S L O W L Y to show that she is being patient. "I know that you're upset. It is very sad. Give it a little time. Eventually you'll feel better." And then she's up, clearing dishes from the table, done.

I need to get out of here before Mom can say another wrong thing about Maybe, something that has more to do with her dealing with a crying-all-the-time daughter and nothing to do with the perfect little dog he is. Was.

"Excuse me," I say, shoving my chair away from the table. Instead of clomping up the stairs, I walk through the kitchen into the mudroom and out the back door. I walk with a longer stride than normal—I need to be away from the house as quickly as possible.

The wind is pretty strong, and I'm reminded that change is coming. Before long, trees will be completely bare and the sky will be that gloomy dirty white of winter. Ugh, walking brings back the fact that I only ever walked around this block with Maybe. Doing it without Maybe is too hard. I turn around and go inside, climb the stairs quietly, so my parents don't hear me, and crawl into my bed.

CHAPTER ELEVEN

I spend Saturday in my room, but Sunday morning, Mom says I have to shower. So I do. Then I go back into my room and close the door.

I've been in there all morning and part of the afternoon when Dad knocks and asks, "Want to take a ride?"

I imagine myself blinking like an animal waking from a not-long-enough hibernation. I do a quick in-my-brain check of homework and even though I haven't done any yet and have enough to qualify as an excuse to say, *Go ask Navy*, instead I say, "Sure. I'll be right there." I'm going to be miserable wherever I am. I may as well take this sad show on the road.

I climb into the truck, fasten my seat belt, and call dibs on the radio.

"You don't get dibs," Dad says, turning it on, volume low. "Let me hear the weather forecast and then you can change it."

"Where are we going?" I ask.

He turns right at the corner and starts heading east. "We

got that new client—a smoke-damage job. I have to drop off a contract.

"Gum?" Dad asks, flipping down his sun visor. He has a complex system of red rubber bands running horizontally and vertically, holding a surprising number of things—gum, pen, nail file, mini-screwdriver, two quarters—in place.

"No thanks."

As we drive east, the homes grow larger and farther apart. Behind these houses, tennis courts, pools, little bathhouses for the pools. A lot of them are summer homes, abandoned for now.

"How are you doing, Army?" Dad asks.

When I've been sad before, it's been about stupid little things—a fight with Navy, a party I wasn't invited to. Talking with Dad helped then. Nothing can fix this. I shrug.

My phone buzzes. I don't recognize the number but the message in all caps makes it pretty clear Elsie Jenkins somehow got my number.

YOU'RE COMING OVER THIS WEEK.

REMEMBER TO HAVE YOUR MOM SEND A NOTE SO YOU CAN RIDE ON MY BUS.

Dad turns to look at me. And then does it again. And again. The kind of thing that would usually make me start to laugh the third or fourth time I felt him do it, but it feels like my emotions are so raw and jumbled that anything that comes out is going to be sadness. Sure enough, tears start falling. I'm not even all-out crying, just pumping out tears.

Dad's not looking at me when he reaches over and squeezes my leg right above the knee. "I know this has been awful. Tell me how you're holding up," he says.

"Not well."

Dad nods, with this sort of sad expression on his face, like he understands. But then he says, "Mom's right, you know. It *will* get easier."

I have no response for that. Everything has changed and the foreverness of it—that weight is too heavy for me.

"Did you hear that?" Dad asks, pressing the button to switch the radio station to my favorite. "It's supposed to be clear and warm all week. I can't remember a fall as mild as this one."

"I'm not sure I believe in weather forecasts," I say. "If they predict a nice week, just watch, a major storm starts pounding us."

He stops at a light and looks at me until I meet his eyes. "Your mother would say that you just said the jinxiest thing she ever heard and now a storm will definitely come."

"*Jinxiest* is not a word," I say.

"Well, it ought to be," Dad says. "I don't believe in jinxes, especially not the way your mother does, but I do know you can't go around acting cavalier about weather, Army. It's like asking a big storm to tear apart your town."

It sounds like he does *too* believe in jinxes. But he's not wrong about Mom's take on jinxes, where it seems like anything you say can cause bad luck—or bad weather.

"I have a strong feeling about this winter," he says, his head shaking slowly. "It's going to be a tough one."

It's impossible to imagine a bad winter right now. The sky is a perfect blue. Just a few puffy, friendly sheep clouds.

" 'And why's that, Dad?' you might ask," Dad says.

"I might," I say. "But I didn't."

"This is the place." He pulls into a driveway on Ocean Avenue and parks the truck in front of a huge white house with big columns. I turn to look past him, across the street, at the beach. The lifeguard chairs—summer's tall, stark guardians—are tipped on their sides for winter. The beach is empty.

"Anyway," Dad says. "All signs point to a tough winter—haven't you seen all the acorns—I don't remember ever raking up so many before. I saw two huge spiderwebs in the basement and there were three woodpeckers all in the same tree . . ."

Holy cow. My dad made me smile. He's so ridiculous. "You're not making this up? Three woodpeckers means a bad winter? What if the fourth one just got lost?"

"Don't mock me! This is real, Army. Those are all signs of a tough winter ahead. Read *The Old Farmer's Almanac* sometime. You'll see." He's memorized one of its lists: Twenty Signs of a Hard Winter.

Dad opens his door and steps out. "It'll only take a sec."

He walks up to the big wooden door and rings the bell. A woman opens it and reaches out to take the papers he's offering her. They talk for a while and then he comes back to the truck.

I don't see any fire damage—it must be in the back or the basement. I'm about to ask him about it when he asks, "Are you in a rush? A lot of homework?"

I shake my head. I don't want to go home sooner than I have to.

Dad motions across the street with a tilt of his head and his eyebrows up, like, *Want to go to the beach?* He knows I do. I love living in a place where going to the beach isn't something you only do in the summer.

He moves the truck and parks it in the empty parking lot. Then we go down the ramp to the sand. I slide my shoes off and then my socks. Dad keeps his on.

I will not think about the insane happiness Maybe always felt when we brought him here. It was the only place he ever barked from pure joy, other than when we played wild animal race. First an openmouthed smile, and then a series of barks and running around and jumping.

My phone buzzes with a text again.

WHICH DAY THIS WEEK?

Elsie Jenkins has to stop.

Dad and I stand there, looking out at the wide beach,

the ocean, all that water. And then we start walking toward it. I picture the beach as it looks in summer, crowded with blankets and striped umbrellas and big picnic coolers, people everywhere, kids digging with brightly colored shovels and pails, lifeguards sitting above everyone, looking out at the water with that important sense of purpose.

Mom used to watch me and Navy so closely when we played in the ocean. One extra-hot day, when I was eight and embarrassed that my mother was the only one *right there*, I said, "The lifeguards are watching, Mom. Go back to our blanket."

"There are so many people in the ocean and just a few lifeguards," she said. "We all need to look out for each other."

I can't stand it. Every thought leads me back to sadness. Looking out for each other. Looking out for Maybe. My one responsibility. And I will pay, forever, for failing at it.

I tell my dad I want to go home.

CHAPTER TWELVE

Mondays are always kind of awful, but I'm living at a whole new level of awfulness now.

My mom has a cousin Alyssa who lives in Texas and sometimes Alyssa decides that she really, really needs to talk to my mom, even if my mom doesn't have time. *Persistent* is the word my mother uses to describe Alyssa. It's almost like a curse word the way Mom says it.

That's what it's been like with Elsie Jenkins. She was persistent. There was no way out of going to her house. So I decided to get it over with. Which makes this like Monday times two.

It's always weird when you take someone else's bus. Like walking into a house that's designed exactly like your house but filled with entirely different things. Yours might be a quiet house that smells like lavender and the identical house could be filled with blaring jazz you've never heard before and the strong smell of cooked fish.

Elsie Jenkins's bus is hotter than mine, and filled with different—but similar—people. We pass eight empty seats before she extends her hand, telling me to sit in the window seat. I try not to think about how much I don't want to be doing this. But it's almost as if I'm in this alternative universe—I don't want to do *anything*.

But I *really* don't want to be hanging out with Elsie Jenkins.

It's so hot, the grossest kind of bus-hot. I try to open the window, to let out some of the sweat smell and let in some breathable air, but it's locked shut. I hope her stop is one of the first.

My phone vibrates—a text from JennaLouise.

I didn't see you just get on the 4 bus with Elsie Jenkins did I?

I turn so Elsie Jenkins can't see the screen.

Thanks to you. Remember how you promised her I'd go over to her house?

JennaLouise responds with a nearly infinite series of laughing emojis. She's kind of evil. And perfect. Except for this. How *did* I end up with Elsie Jenkins???

Out on the street, we pass Johnny on the Spot lifting something into his truck. It's not taking a lot of effort—he has it over his head. Oh. A giant stuffed panda—the white spots are kind of dark and not-clean looking. What could he want a ratty stuffed animal for?

Is it weird that Elsie Jenkins and I aren't talking? Everyone else on the bus is. What can I talk about with her?

She reaches up to her neck and pulls out a worn leather cord that's tucked inside her shirt. Dangling off it is a giant ring. It looks like one of those big ugly rings professional athletes wear when they win a championship. She catches me staring. "Sorry," I say, because it feels like I've seen something I wasn't meant to see.

"It was my dad's high school ring." She cradles the silver in her right hand.

I envision a giant man, maybe a lumberjack (it's a really big ring), wearing a Clay Coves High School varsity jacket. I wonder what he does.

"He died when I was eight," she says.

In the time it took Elsie Jenkins to say those words, just six words, gravity grew stronger. I feel it, a force pulling me right through the springy bus seat all the way down toward the center of the earth. Because that is the worst sentence in the world. *He died when I was eight.* I think of my own dad. And try to picture life, my family's life, without him, but I literally can't. My imagination won't allow it. I feel the weight of Maybe's death like a massive pile of wet wool sweaters I carry with me everywhere, but a dad. A dad who died. I can't even.

"Did he give it to you?" I ask. I picture her giant lumberjack father wanting his daughter to always know how much he loves her, giving her something important, something that's all him becoming something that's all hers.

"No, my mom did. On my ninth birthday." Her fingers

work the leathery knot until it opens. She slides the ring off and holds it in her palm.

I had been thinking of Elsie Jenkins as the persistent girl who always wears tan. And now when I look at this same Elsie Jenkins all I see is her father in her palm—a big, gaudy piece of silver, dulled a bit with blackness and time.

"Do you always wear it?"

She nods. "He loved to surf."

"That is so cool," I say. Because surfing just is. But I'd probably have said it even if she'd said, *He loved to cut people's arms off,* because her father is dead and it's important to somehow honor him and his life. I kind of wonder how he died, but it doesn't seem like I can ask. "Do you remember a lot about him?"

"Not enough." She gently rubs her finger around the outside of the ring before putting it back on the leather and reaching up to tie it around her neck. "He smelled like almonds." She sighs and leans her head back against the seat.

If Elsie Jenkins's mother were my mom, she wouldn't have that ring. It would have been neatly filed away in a box marked JEWELRY, stacked on a high shelf in some closet that was rarely opened.

My mom actually has a sign over her work desk that, when she bought it, said OUT WITH THE OLD AND IN WITH THE NEW. Mom crossed out the last four words and wrote OUT WITH THE OLD again in blue marker. It makes her laugh every time she looks at it, but I don't get what's funny about it.

We get off the bus right in front of Elsie Jenkins's house and it turns out it's actually just a few blocks from my house, but it's at the top of the hill on the other side of Cold Spring Boulevard, the dividing line for elementary schools. It's close, but I never knew her, or very many other people from Towne Elementary, until we all started sixth grade at Clay Coves Intermediate School last year.

"My mom's still, um, at work," she says, looking at me funny. And that's when my brain makes the connection. Dr. Jenkins/Elsie Jenkins. Elsie Jenkins's mother is our vet.

The vet who was there when the worst thing that could ever happen happened.

Why did I agree to this? What was I thinking?

I have no choice but to follow her into the house.

"Do you want something to eat?" she asks, leading me through a short hallway to a kitchen.

"I'm not really hungry," I say.

"Then let's go to my room." She pulls her phone from her back pocket. "I just have to text my mom that I'm home."

I follow her up the stairs. Her bedroom is small and it looks like something out of a magazine or TV decorator show or my mom's fantasy life. Not one thing is out of place. The book next to her bed isn't thrown on the floor with tissues all around it. It's sitting on her nightstand, closed, with a neat bookmark sticking out the top. Her desk has folders on it, like in an office.

"I'm glad you wanted to come over," she says. That's kind of tricky language she's using there. Elsie Jenkins didn't really give me much of a choice. I can't think of an honest thing to say in response so I just stand there.

Whatever is seven steps beyond awkward is what this is.

I look around at the neatness.

I wait.

It's painful.

"So with the PTA, we fill out this form," she says, pulling it out of a desk drawer, "and once the school approves the program, they'll give us a petition and we need to get fifty kids' signatures. And we send that to the PTA and they make the decision. Service with a Wag would be a good organization to support and I think everyone would love to see those dogs, don't you?"

"Yeah," I say. "Everyone would definitely rather watch an assembly than sit in class. But I don't really get how having them do a presentation is supporting them."

She reaches for a tissue and blows her nose so loudly that I think she's kidding. She's not.

"The PTA would pay them, giving money to that organization, and it's an organization that helps people." She blows her nose again, not quite as loud this time. "It feels good to help people."

"It's what my parents do, so I know about helping people," I say.

"Oh, I know what your parents do is important. My mom's work's sometimes like that too." And then she looks at me in a way that means she knows everything. *Oh God, no. I cannot melt. Not here. No.*

She may understand I need a minute, because she says, "I'm hungry. Are you sure you don't want anything? Pretzels? Chips?"

"No thanks. But, um, where's your bathroom?" We walk out of the bedroom and she points me to the right, then heads downstairs.

There are pictures all over the wall. Some are of little Elsie Jenkins sitting on the shoulders of a man who must be her father. Ah, she's wearing lots of blue and red! Medium Elsie Jenkins in green, standing in front of both of her parents. Elsie Jenkins as she's looked since I've known her, wearing tan from head to toe. All by herself. I stare at one of the pictures of Elsie Jenkins with her dad for a while.

On a ledge below the family photos are loose pictures of animals, mostly dogs and cats. One of them looks just like . . . oh, no way, one of them is! It's Maybe! Baby Maybe! Tears start welling up because holy cow, he was so cute. He's tucked between pictures of a pair of black pugs and an orange kitten. I never saw this picture before! It's like how cute Maybe was, only times infinity because of how cute puppies are—it's the cutest thing I have ever seen.

I have no control over what happens, over what my hands do. They reach out, take the picture, and tuck it into my back pocket. I steal the photo from Elsie Jenkins and her mother, and I don't even feel bad because it's not like it's something I want to do. It's something my body just *did,* it was need, not want, and there are all these other pets there anyway and

Elsie Jenkins and her mother won't miss this one picture of this one puppy and really, I bet if I asked they'd say yes, but I can't ask because that would open it all up, how Maybe's not even a dog who exists anymore on account of what I did and really, it won't hurt them at all, not having this picture, one of many, many pictures, and I need it. I just do.

I also need to get away. I forget all about the bathroom. I grab my backpack and walk downstairs to the kitchen and like I'm a liar with all kinds of lying-liar experience, I say, "Hey, I'm really sorry—my mom texted and I need to get home. I'll see you at school, okay?"

"But we didn't even fill out the form yet," she says. "I mean, you just got here."

"I'm sorry, Elsie Jenkins, but I have to go." I walk out the door and head toward home, the picture letting off something like heat in my back pocket.

CHAPTER THIRTEEN

I cross Cold Spring Boulevard and pass Mr. Hoffart's house and see that his newspaper's not at the top of his driveway again. He must be wondering why the delivery guy stopped bringing it to his door. One more thing to feel bad about.

Lots of homes are decorated with pumpkins and bales of hay. Plastic ghosts hang from trees and blow in the wind. But it's so warm. The air is the kind you feel when you step back onto the sand after a long summer swim in the ocean. Its weight wraps around you like a towel.

As I turn the corner onto Marigold Street, I see the new neighbor pushing a double stroller and walking with her daughter, Madison.

"Hi there, Army," she says. "It's such a beautiful day, I needed to get out of the—"

She's interrupted by the painfully loud sound of screeching brakes. The recycling truck pulls up in front of the house we're standing near. One baby is asleep and one is getting fussy. Madison covers her ears. She looks like she might be in pain.

I'm trying not to stare, but all at once she's losing it.

She's rocking back and forth. And then Madison's sitting on the ground, hands still covering her ears, kicking the air.

"Army, can I ask for a huge favor?" the mother says.

I nod.

"This could take a while," she says. "I was heading home to give Schuyler his bottle. It's in a warmer on the kitchen table. Can you bring him home and give it to him? And I guess you should take Tyler too. Would that be okay?"

I nod. But what I'd like to say is, *I'd like more training first, please.* There are pictures of little-kid me giving Navy a bottle, so I'm sure no special skills are required, but these babies don't know me. Madison's mom doesn't seem too concerned; she steps aside so I can take the stroller.

Madison is still kicking the air and now she's making a sound. It's not a word. And it's not happy. Her mom just sits down next to her.

I look in the stroller and quickly ask, "Which one gets the bottle?"

If I were the mom, that might be a clue that this is not the person to trust with my two babies. But she just says, "Schuyler, the one with a pacifier," and turns to Madison.

Back at their house, I leave the stroller outside on the stoop, unstrap the first baby and put him in this little playpen in their living room, and then I get the kid with the pacifier.

The house looks so different from when the Rooneys lived here. Boxes are stacked everywhere except for the places where there's baby stuff. Tons of baby stuff. I walk into the kitchen and find the bottle. I sit on a kitchen chair and try to hold the baby on my lap, but somehow we don't fit, so I carry him to the living room and sit on the couch with him. He takes the rubbery part of the bottle right into his mouth and starts sucking. No instructions required.

The other baby, Tyler, is lying on his back in the playpen, trying to shove a big red block into his mouth. He's making little baby sounds and seems pretty happy. After fifteen minutes of Tyler's *kaaaa*s and *gaaaa*s, and the drinking baby growing heavier in my lap, the front door opens.

Madison walks in with her mom. Madison's looking straight ahead but her mom is looking right at me. I don't know what the look on my face says, but the one on hers says something like *holy cow*. Not the *wow! I won a contest!* kind of holy cow. Another kind.

I wish there was a not-rude way to ask her to explain to me about Madison. My parents have drilled it into my head that you don't ask other people about their private business. If they decide to tell you about their lives, that's fine and you listen carefully.

So I'm just going to listen carefully and hope that Madison's mom answers the questions I can't ask: *What happened just now? Does it happen a lot?*

She reaches for the baby and as he's leaving my arms for hers, he spits up some of the milk or formula or whatever he just drank, and it falls right on the carpet.

"Of course," their mom says. "I'll get that in a minute.

You are a top-of-the-line good neighbor, Army. Thank you for helping me."

"You're welcome," I say.

"Can I just ask you one thing? I am so terrible with names. I've met lots of neighbors and the only name I remember is yours. Could you be my secret name helper? Like the family in the blue house—the woman's name is Gloria? They invited us to trick-or-treat with them and I can't remember their names."

"It's Laura," I say. "And Steve. And their kids are Stevie and Bella."

"Right. Great. And just one more thing. Do you know the name of the people with the house behind ours? Their backyard and ours meet? It's a white house with red shutters."

"The McNeals," I say. Mrs. McNeal used to sometimes invite Maybe into their yard to race around with her two Dalmatians whose Shakespeare-y names are the only neighborhood-dog names I can never remember. I don't mention that right now, since I'm busy becoming some kind of name hero. And also, no. No Maybe memories, please.

"You might be my secret weapon, Army. Do you think I could have your cell number, hon? So I can call you when my brain goes blank? You've lived here a long time, right?" She starts looking through a pile of stuff on a shelf right inside the door.

"All my life," I say. "But listen, this is sort of embarrassing but . . ."

"No. I just admitted I don't know anyone's name but yours, so whatever you need to say, just say it."

"I don't know *your* name."

The woman lets out a big laugh. A friendly one. "You know I have a daughter who sneaks out of my house and back in my window, and well, really, you've seen Madison pull everything she has out of the autism playbook already and I never thought to tell you my name. It's Irene. I just need to find a piece of paper to write your number down. I can never find anything. Ever."

I nod, then ask, "Do you have your phone?"

"I should," she says, "but I'm not sure where."

I pull out mine. "What's your number? I'll text you."

Irene looks at me blankly.

This isn't obvious? "And then my number will be on your phone."

"You are one smart girl. Maybe you'll really be my secret weapon. An Army of one."

CHAPTER FOURTEEN

I cross the street and walk toward my house, the picture of Maybe still practically burning in my back pocket. Johnny on the Spot's truck is parked in Linda and Sue's driveway. The women, our neighbors two doors down, are standing in the bed of the truck, leaning over a box, arguing. Johnny on the Spot's sitting in the cab—it looks like he's reading the newspaper.

Their voices are loud. "We can't, Linda, so I don't know why you told him we could."

"If we don't, they die, Sue. I can't live with that. Oh, hey, Army."

They stand there, looking down at me. I was hoping to walk into my house unnoticed. I'm pretty sure no one wants some random neighbor overhearing their argument.

"Want to take a look?" Linda asks.

"At what?" I don't walk any closer because there are certain things, like, say, rats and snakes and the hairy kind of spider, that I don't even want to be near.

"Come up and see."

I've always been a dog person. But when I climb onto the truck bed and peek into the box, I get a glimpse of why some people are cat people. Tiny kittens. Two orange, three gray. Mewing. Mewling. In small little voices that make my heart hurt a tiny bit.

"Where's their mother?" I ask. It's pretty clear that creatures this tiny still need to be with their mama.

"We have no idea," Linda says. "She's gone."

"And we don't care," Sue says. "Because we don't have the time to raise five kittens and you know it, Linda. And I can't stand the heartache over the ones we lose."

Of course she can't. It's the hardest thing in the world.

"It's not like Johnny chose to find them," Linda says. "And we've done it before." Linda's hands are in the box, her index finger stroking the head of one kitten after another.

I wait for Sue's argument, but she just says, "That's true. We have." She sounds tired but there's a hint of something that makes me look away from the kittens and into her face. Which has a little smile.

"So how did they end up here?" I ask.

"You know the way people call your parents if they've had storm damage or a flood or whatever?" Sue says. "We're sort of like that, with cats." She turns to Linda and says, "You win. Let's tell Johnny we'll take them."

Linda nods. And she's smiling.

I knew people called Linda and Sue *the cat ladies*, but I never thought about where all the cats came from.

"Good luck," I say.

I'm about to jump down from the truck when Sue reaches out and holds on to my upper arm. "Hey," she says. "I was really sorry to hear about Maybe. He was such a good dog. It's really hard to lose a pet."

My mouth is stuck in a stupid O. I can't tell Sue that it's something I can't talk about yet. And also there's something so weird, so grown-up, about someone mentioning a death to you, offering condolences or whatever, and there must be some grown-up way I'm supposed to respond. The best I can do is to whisper, "Thanks." I step down into their driveway.

As I head home, I try to replace the Maybe's-dead-and-also-it-was-my-fault thoughts with images of the tiny ears, tails, paws in that box. I hope the kittens will all be okay.

I'm closing the front door when a big green van turns into Irene's driveway. Goldsmith the Locksmith.

Inside, Mom's drinking coffee and reading something. She looks up at me with her head tilted to the side, almost like Maybe when he hoped I was doing something—giving him a new toy, taking him for a walk at a weird time—that I didn't usually do. "How was it? What's her name again, the girl whose house you were at?"

"Okay," I say. "And Elsie Jenkins. She's Dr. Jenkins's daughter."

"Why didn't you call when you were done? I could have picked you up."

I shrug. "I felt like walking."

“That sounds like a step in the right direction,” Mom says with a smile.

It doesn’t feel like one. But the truth—how I stole a photo of Maybe and had to get out of Elsie Jenkins’s house immediately—isn’t exactly something that would make my mother happy. So I just shrug and walk upstairs to my room.

CHAPTER FIFTEEN

I turn on the computer and read a little about autism. It says that autistic people's brains work differently, and that the brain and senses don't always communicate so well, which can affect their social skills. That makes me think of the autistic people I've known in school and my cousin's next-door neighbor Will.

Then I find a section about nonverbal autism, which sounds like Madison and might explain why she doesn't talk. It says there hasn't been enough research and no one fully understands the thought processes of nonverbal autistic people.

I do learn some stuff though, like how autism can tie into people's senses—that they feel/see/hear/taste/touch too much or not enough or both, which is probably what happened with Madison and that noisy recycling truck. Some autistic people are undersensitive to touch, and a lot of those people like to burrow under piles of blankets the way I do. These days, being underneath the blankets, I don't have to pretend that I don't have a gigantic hole at the center of my very self. (A hole that is the same exact shape as Maybe.) There's even an article about how some autistic kids walk away from their homes by themselves because they have an impaired sense of danger.

There's a knock on my door and then I hear Navy's voice. "Army? I have something."

Navy?

"Yeah, okay, come in," I say, climbing onto my bed.

"This is for you," Navy says, walking in with a box. "But now I'm thinking it might be a bad idea. You can give it back if you don't want it."

I think of something Dad says when he comes upon something puzzling: *What have we here?* The only time Navy and I give each other things is on our birthdays and Christmas, and only because our parents make us.

He steps over the small polka-dot rug and places the box on my bed.

"Open it," he says.

I do.

And inside: *Oh. Oh. Just wow. Oh wow. Oh.*

Maybe's leash. His bowl. The orange tin for his favorite treats. His red collar. Even his little green ball, the one he loved to hold in his mouth while running in proud circles around the coffee table in the living room. The very things Mom threw away—everything that was gone the morning after he died.

"Mom threw all this stuff out," I say.

"I know. Can I?" he asks, motioning that he wants to sit on my bed.

"Of course. But I mean, how did you get it?"

"From the garbage. For you. I don't know. I thought you'd want it maybe."

"Maybe," I say, my heart cracking.

Just then my hand, reaching around in the box, hits something achingly familiar. My fingers melt into the texture. ZippyPaws dog! Maybe's sweet blue dog, almost like a stuffed animal, but with ropy parts to chew. I pull it from the box and am flooded, just flooded. When Navy sees the tears, he winces and hangs his head. "I'm sorry," he says, almost whispers.

"No, Navy. No. This is the best thing," I say. "I mean, you didn't make me cry. Or I guess you did, but in the best way. I love that you saved these things. I love that you did this."

And I do. I've needed things my eyes could look at and my fingers could touch and hold. "I'm always thinking about him," I say. "That's really what I'm trying to say." I reach for a tissue because I am so gross in the nose, and I blow it almost as loud as Elsie Jenkins did and for some reason that makes me hiccup. That makes Navy laugh, and just like that, he's no longer slouched with worry and guilt.

"You know what I mean, don't you? The crying—yeah, I'm sad. But I'm always sad about Maybe. And now you gave me a way to... well, now I can..." I sort through the box again, thinking about Maybe but also about Navy. He's just a little kid. He laughs when people say *fart*. "How did you know to do this? How come *I* didn't know to do this?"

He shrugs.

Mom was just doing what my parents always do—packing up the signs of disaster. Out with the old and out with the old. How did this little punk kid know to do the exact opposite? And how could he—why would he—when the whole horrible thing was my fault?

He must not know.

"I don't really deserve this," I say, closing the box. "Did you know it was my fault? That Maybe ate chocolate cupcakes I made with JennaLouise and that's why he died? It's all my fault."

"Remember when me and Owen left the back gate open and Maybe got out?"

I'd forgotten, but yeah. We didn't even know Maybe was gone until he showed up at the front door, barking.

"I was so upset," he said, "because of what could have happened." He looks like he's afraid of me—of making me cry again, maybe?

"But all that mattered was that nothing happened. Maybe was fine," I say.

"Yeah," Navy says. "But that was the same kind of thing, right? That time we were lucky and this time we—well, anyway, I thought you might want this stuff."

I open the box and touch everything again. "Seriously,

Navy. This is the nicest thing anyone's ever done for me. Thank you."

"I did it for me too," he says. "But more for you."

I lean over and pull him close into a hug. It's bizarre and a little revolting and doesn't feel natural or even good, but it is what I need to do.

He lets me and then races out of the room.

CHAPTER SIXTEEN

I used to love being home alone when Maybe was here. Now it just makes his absence more obvious, like a bright spotlight shining where Maybe used to be but isn't anymore.

Navy's at a friend's house and my parents are each out running errands. And my very soul is being impaled by these miserable two pages of word problems. I could live with straight-up math. But it's so hard to concentrate on how many weeks it will take for Christopher to have enough money if he wants to buy a comic book that costs $11, a dictionary that costs $22, and a dozen cookies that cost $2.25 each, if his allowance is $12 per week and he's been spending half of it each week on potato chips. I have so many issues with this math problem, but mostly I can't get past the idea of Christopher buying himself a dictionary. Use an online dictionary, Christopher.

I cannot concentrate.

At all.

So I run down to the kitchen, find a probably too-old apple and cut it up for a snack, carving out the gross parts.

I listen to a song I've been humming lately but haven't heard since fourth grade. I even put away all my laundry. I think of running another load but it's only Wednesday and I usually save that for Saturday.

Then—and this is progress—I sit down at my desk.

But I stand right back up and find the jeans I wore to Elsie Jenkins's house. I take the picture I stole from the pocket and stare at it until my eyes grow blurry. I put it in the box Navy gave me.

Out the window, I see a person. But my brain takes its time realizing that it's not just a person. What I am looking at is a person on a roof. A person, a little person, standing on the roof of a house. Madison. I grab my phone to call Irene, but it's dead, so I race downstairs, leaping two and three steps at a time.

The roof, or whatever you call that mini-balcony over Madison's house's front door, is flat but that doesn't make it less scary to see her standing there, so far above the ground.

Outside I feel like I need to run hard toward their house but maybe I should tiptoe so I don't scare Madison if she sees me. I take large steps slowly, evenly.

I push the doorbell and when no one answers I ring it again and again.

The door opens slowly, like no big deal, and Irene says, "Army?"

"Madison's on your roof!!"

Irene's eyes go wide. She steps out of the house and looks up. "Oh my God. She was just here! I was in the bathroom. I mean, how did—"

Irene seems stuck. I practically push her back inside. Then she finds her momentum, keeps moving, starts running up the stairs. I follow her into a room that has a big bed and not much else in it, then through to another room with a desk. There's a chair next to the open window. Irene walks over and leans out. "Madison," she says. "Come inside."

Madison doesn't move.

"Army? Can you stay a while, honey? Listen for the twins. They should be waking up soon."

"Um, okay."

Irene sticks her leg out the window, then pulls herself through.

I go downstairs and sit on the couch. I look around the room. Almost everything is low to the ground except the shelves, which are bolted to the wall. On the coffee table there are bills or forms or both—tons of papers—all spread out. My hands are shaking, my heart racing. My mouth is dry. I make myself sit and try to take deep breaths.

Can I make myself think about Christopher's quest for a new dictionary? No.

I sit and hope, hope, hope: *Please don't let me hear any terrifying sounds like the kind someone might make when falling off a roof.*

Should I call 911? But wait. Sirens? Sirens are louder than

a recycling truck. Is there such a thing as a no-siren emergency vehicle?

I start pacing and peek into the room that Mrs. Rooney used as her craft room. It's filled with taped-up cardboard boxes, tons of them lining the walls.

A baby starts crying loudly. I run up the stairs and into the room the noise is coming from and find a red-faced Schuyler or Tyler, sputtering, ramping up to screaming. I reach to lift him out, but he pulls away with a hard jerk, bumping the back of his head on the side of the crib. His face screws up into a tight little mask of fire-hot anger, pure fury, and he lets out a ferocious howl. I reach for him again but he pulls away and he's turning red so I run to the room that leads out to the roof.

I stick my head out the window. Irene is sitting with Madison, and they're as far from the edge as they can be.

"The baby," I say. "He got hurt."

Irene's not listening.

I can practically hear my mother telling me to get another adult to help. But this can't wait. I take the deepest breath I can, put my leg out the window, and step onto the roof. "Go. I'll stay here."

Irene looks like she's not understanding.

"The baby's crying and he pulled away when I was trying to get him and he hit his head. He's not going to let me get him out of that crib—he needs you. Really. I can sit here with Madison. I can do this."

Irene starts to object but before she can say anything, I

add, "The baby might really be hurt. I promise to be so careful until you get back." She seems frozen until she shakes her head and then disappears inside.

I actually think the words, *Here I am. On a roof.* Like I'm some kind of easy-to-read book.

It's only one story off the ground, but it feels like so much more.

I will be so careful.

Madison is still, calm, looking out over the houses.

It's an interesting way to look at Marigold Street, to take in more of it at once, to be as high up as where the tree branches start shooting in different directions. Why am I thinking almost normal thoughts when I am in the most not-normal situation there has ever been?

Should I be trying to convince Madison to come inside? What if she moves? And then falls? What if I fall trying to grab her, feet over head over feet?

A breeze blows Madison's hair back from her face. Her eyes look straight out, and she's rocking a little. She doesn't seem unhappy.

"Hey, Madison, do you want to go inside?" She doesn't respond.

Irene sticks her head out and asks, "You two doing okay?" It seems more like something a mom yells downstairs when you're hanging in the basement watching *The Wizard of Oz* or playing video games. *You doing okay? Want some popcorn?* Not so much when you're as scared as I am.

Without getting an answer, Irene says, "I just need one more minute. Make sure you stay away from the edges." She pulls her head back inside.

I can't just sit here doing nothing. It makes every minute last longer, somehow. So I start talking.

"I used to have a dog. Maybe," I say, peeking to see if Madison gives any sign that she is listening to me.

"I didn't mean to name him Maybe. But my family has a history of accidental names." I'm about to tell the whole story of how Mary became Army but no, my mouth has other ideas. "Whenever I asked my mother if we could have a dog, she said *maybe,* but we kept not getting a dog. And then I thought it was funny to pretend that I thought the dog I was getting was named Maybe. When we actually got him, I couldn't imagine calling him anything else.

"But he died, Madison. It'll be a week tomorrow."

Madison shifts a little, wrapping her arms around her bent legs, leaning her upper body forward into the wind.

"It's been so awful. It was my fault that he died and that will always be true. I'm having a hard time with *always.* And *forever.*"

If you take away the fact that she's on a roof, you'd probably only notice how calm Madison looks.

"It might not be obvious that I'm all broken apart," I say. "Most people probably can't see the cracks from the outside."

And then—what changes?—Madison stands.

What do I do? Scream at her to sit? Before my brain can

stagger back to life, Madison moves in front of me. She grabs my arm and pulls me toward the window. She steps inside. I follow and shut the window behind me. Madison goes through the little room and the room with just a bed, out to the hall, and down the stairs. At the bottom, about to head up the stairs, is Irene, holding a baby. She turns and we all go into the living room. The baby looks okay, not too lumpy or bumpy or broken.

"Okay, then," Irene says with a big deep sigh. "Okay." She nods. "Phew."

Madison stands with her back against a bookshelf, quiet.

"The locksmith put locks on most of the windows, including the one Madison climbed out of," Irene says, standing and placing Schuyler or possibly Tyler into some round bouncy thing. "We've always known that she can figure out how to open dead bolts and window latches and most locks—she's a magician that way—but we had to try. And we don't want to be restrictive, to keep her from doing what she needs to do, but we have to make sure she's safe. It's a difficult balance and I keep worrying about what if there's a fire. The locksmith said the next step might be alarms on all the doors and windows. But Madison doesn't do well with loud sounds so maybe we'll try one that sends alerts to our phones. Kyle hasn't been home much, but when he gets back from his business trip, we're going to have to figure something out."

I can't think of a single response.

"You're a godsend to me, Army. Thank you."

"Oh," I say. "No. I mean, you're welcome."

"Wherever we've been, there's always been someone. When Madison was born, we lived near my parents. They practically lived with us when we realized Madison needed constant attention. Then the twins surprised us and we had to move to North Carolina for Kyle's work and there was this family next door, our closest friends, the Estins, who also have an autistic child. Anyway, it was like we were all one family, everyone looking out for each other. And now, here in Clay Coves, we found you. I'm so grateful you saw Madison on the roof."

It's nice, what Irene's saying, but it hits me like a giant wave I didn't see coming. If all she has in Clay Coves is me, she's in trouble.

Just then, Madison walks over to me. She grabs my arm and tugs, pulling me, trying to get me to go with her. She says something that sounds like "Uh" and keeps pulling. I look at Irene.

"She wants you to go with her," she says.

I get that, but . . .

Madison pulls me by the arm into the kitchen. She says *uh* over and over, and goes to stand by the refrigerator. Then she says it louder. "Uh! Uh!"

I want to cry. It's so clear that Madison is telling me she wants something but I have no idea what. None. It seems cruel, not giving Madison whatever it is she wants.

Irene is watching from the doorway. "Wow. She really likes you. She's asking you for pink jelly beans."

How did Irene know that the *uh* sound means pink jelly beans?

Irene walks past us, reaches up to the cabinet, and grabs a giant bag of pink jelly beans. She counts three into Madison's hands.

Madison shoves them in her mouth and puts her hand back out.

"Later," her mother says.

So Madison uses sounds to let people know what she wants. But that can't work for all the things she wants or what she's feeling. It must be so hard for Irene too. Even though she just did some kind of magic translation in which a one-syllable sound was a clear request for pink jelly beans.

"Thanks again," Irene says, which might be my signal to leave. "I really hope we won't keep needing you to save us from emergencies. And I promise, things aren't as bad as they look."

CHAPTER SEVENTEEN

Mom's car and Dad's truck still aren't in the driveway and thank goodness. I don't want to talk to anyone right now. All I want to do is go straight upstairs to the linen closet and throw every extra blanket on my bed and burrow to the bottom. That house is like a pirate ship in the Wild West with some germy Chuck E. Cheese kids thrown in and it really feels like some horrible, can't-go-back tragedy is going to happen.

I walk in the front door and before I can even have an I'm-home-and-all-is-safe-for-now second to myself, I hear the sound of water gurgling in pipes and Mom calling, "Army, where were you?"

Oh no. Mom's home. "I was at Irene's," I yell.

"Can't hear you," Mom calls loudly. This is one of many annoying things she does. Instead of, say, stepping closer, she calls out that she can't hear and expects me to move closer. So I do, through the living room and the dining room and then the kitchen, because it will be better to get this over with quickly. But that heavy pile of soft, warm, weighty blankets upstairs is really calling to me.

Mom's in the mudroom, big green rubber gloves up to her elbows, cleaning out the bailing buckets. It's Dad's job to keep them clean, but sometimes she decides they're not clean enough. (Don't ask me why bailing buckets need to be clean. I have no idea.) She's like an efficient machine, doing the work without having to pay attention—grab, pour water, rinse, swirl, dump, rinse, swirl, dump, next bucket.

"Where were you?" she asks again.

What I wouldn't give to be under that pile of blankets! "At Irene's. Where's your car?"

"At the shop, getting new tires. Who's Irene?"

"Madison's mom, the new people in the Rooneys' house." I grab rags from the utility closet, pick up a bucket Mom's already rinsed, and wipe it dry.

"Irene? Isn't that a little informal?" Mom adds a bucket to the clean pile and reaches for another dirty one.

"She said to call her Irene and I don't even know their last name."

Mom makes the that's-not-how-we-do-things face. "And what were you doing?" She opens the back door and places a stack of washed-and-dried buckets on the stoop to put back in the garage.

I can still see the rows of gray shingles, the view from up there, the peace Madison seemed to feel being up and away from things—the way she just looked out, her body mostly still while my heart was racing. But I can't mention that Madison was on the roof. And that for a little while, I was up on that roof too. There is no way to tell Mom that won't make her freak out. But I also can't think of anything I can say that's not lying.

"Things are kind of complicated there," I say finally. I reach for a washed bucket and wipe around the rim. "She has those two little babies, and you didn't meet Madison, but she . . ."

"Does she want you to babysit?" Mom asks. Swirl, swirl, dump, rinse. "That might be a good way to take your mind off . . . things."

"Not exactly," I say. I put down the bucket and reach for another. "She just needed some help. And I tried to help."

"Well, that's very nice," Mom says. Something makes her turn off the water and look directly at me. She puts the bucket in the sink.

There's a kindness in her face that I'm not expecting and it makes something tip, start to spill, and the truth I was determined to hold in comes pouring out like a blast of water from a busted pipe. "They're in such a bad place, Mom. I think maybe the dad's not there enough and the babies are babies and they need all this attention, but Madison has kind of serious needs too, and so today when I saw Madison on the roof of their house—"

"What?"

"I know. It was so scary. And Irene seems like she's in real trouble there, Mom, you know? I think she's got way more than she can handle."

Mom pauses—it should be noted that my mom hardly pauses, ever—and puts her hand on my wrist, a hand-to-wrist hug. Her green rubber fingers leave circle marks on my sleeve.

I look from the glove to Mom's face and see something like the look she'd give little me when I stood in the doorway of her bedroom after a nightmare and I think, okay, maybe everything will be okay. And then she talks.

"It doesn't sound like a safe place for you to be. I understand why you want to try to help," she says. "It's what we do, but—"

"No, Mom. If there was a way to help them, I wouldn't want it to be the kind of help we do, mostly after something awful has *already* happened. I want to do better than that. And it's not like there's a box of supplies that will make everything better for them."

She looks like I've slapped her across the face. Hurt. Shocked. But mostly hurt.

"It's my job to look out for you," Mom says. "And that doesn't sound like a safe and stable environment."

I turn and go upstairs.

"Army?" Mom calls up the stairs. "I don't think we're done discussing this."

I pretend not to hear. I definitely need to discuss this. But not with Mom. I go to the linen closet, grab those blankets, bring them to my bed, and burrow in.

CHAPTER EIGHTEEN

The next day after school. My phone buzzes.

A text from JennaLouise:

Mom has to meet client near your house. Can't stay long but I'm coming over!

JennaLouise and I didn't have lunch together today because I wanted to work on something for Art, so I'm practically buzzing with the need to talk to someone about Madison. Yay, Daphne!

Last night I avoided my mother, explaining that math-problem Christopher and I needed to spend a lot of time together if I was going to pass Math. And luckily, she's been out since I got home from school today—she left a note that she was picking up Navy and running some errands.

It's JennaLouise's first time here since, well, since everything. And I kind of want to hug her because of how careful she's being. Like she was about to step around the water bowl, which is no longer there, then glanced down, looked at me, and tried to pretend nothing happened.

We sit at the kitchen table. "Do you have any more of that brown juice?" she asks.

And then I just do it. I hug her.

She reaches out and hugs me back. "I won't ask if you're doing okay, even though I want to."

"Thank you," I say. "So remember the Rooneys, I helped them pack up because they were moving?"

"The little old people?" she asks. That seems like an unkind way to describe them, but also accurate.

"Anyway, these new people moved in."

She leans her head in the general direction of Madison's house. "Did you get your wish for some kids our age? Maybe a cute guy?"

I laugh. "If I remember right, that was your wish."

"I know."

Where should I begin with Madison and her brothers and her mom? "I'm not sure what the opposite of a cute guy is, but—"

"Marcus!" she says, and starts sniffing. Since first grade Marcus has always been in class with me or JennaLouise and he has always been a sniffer. He sniffs *everything*! But I half squirm when I realize what I'm doing—reducing someone to one simple thing. Marcus the sniffer. Elsie Jenkins always wearing tan. Madison is autistic. How would someone reduce me? Army—she's sad. Or she's a dog murderer, maybe.

"I've met the new people—well, most of them—and it's kind of crazy intense. The oldest kid, Madison, is younger than Navy and she doesn't talk."

JennaLouise looks at me, waiting for me to explain. I wish I knew how.

"She's autistic," I say, feeling this little guilt-ache, a pang of regret, just from saying the word, summarizing Madison's whole self with eight letters, but I don't know how else to describe the way she is. "And there are twin baby boys."

"Actually, *do* you have brown juice? I'm really thirsty."

I check the refrigerator but there is nothing. I get her a glass of water, which is safer than brown juice anyway.

"There's a lot I can't figure out. Like I've only met them a few times, but each time was sort of an emergency and I happened to be in the right place to help. So I wonder—was it just weird timing, and things are actually okay, and I've coincidentally been there the few times when things have gotten out of control or . . . I don't know. Is it always out of control? I worry about them."

I tell her about seeing Madison up in the tree and walking in the street by herself.

"How could the mother let her do that?"

"Well, it has to be hard to watch someone every minute of every day, right?" I say. "Especially when she has two babies. They take a lot of time too."

"Then she needs to, I don't know, fix it somehow. Get some help."

That's just how I feel, but hearing JennaLouise say it makes me feel really uncomfortable. It makes me feel a need to protect them. Defend them. So I decide not to mention Madison being up on the roof. It would make JennaLouise think Irene is a horrible mother for sure. And she's not. I hardly know her, but I know she's not.

JennaLouise can't let it go. "A little girl, out by herself in the street? Can you imagine what could happen to her?" JennaLouise watches a lot of *Law & Order* reruns with Margaret Ann.

I don't have to imagine—I saw it. And JennaLouise is right. It's scary. "My mother doesn't want me to go there anymore, but I don't see how I can not help them when they need it, right?"

JennaLouise gives me this look. If I weren't so serious, I might laugh, because I've seen JennaLouise's mom give that same look to her daughters—most recently when Margaret Ann asked if she could get a Teletubbies tattoo. (The red one. Po.)

I thought talking this out with JennaLouise would help me . . . I don't even know what. But it's not only not working, it's making me feel worse. I don't want to talk about it with JennaLouise anymore. And if I can't talk about it with my best friend, then what?

My phone buzzes and I check. Text from Elsie Jenkins.

SEE YOU SUNDAY MORNING AT BEACH CLEANUP!

YOU HAVE TO COME!

STARTS AT 10.

I open my mouth to tell JennaLouise about Elsie Jenkins, but change my mind. "Let's go to my room," I say. Different room, different conversation.

CHAPTER NINETEEN

In the locker-slamming noise of the hallway, JennaLouise and I grab our lunches and head to the cafeteria. "I can't believe it's finally Friday," she says. "Every day I get like an hour of math homework and there's that big science project and it just feels like school is getting harder every day and I am so glad to have two days without sitting in a stupid classroom."

When we get to our table in the cafeteria, someone's already sitting there.

Elsie Jenkins.

"Huh!" JennaLouise says. Just that. *Huh!*

"Hey," I say. I make sure there's nothing but friendliness in my voice because that *huh* from JennaLouise sounded a little mean.

"Good. You're here. I'll go get my lunch now." And then Elsie Jenkins is gone.

JennaLouise shifts into some kind of things-are-not-quite-right slow motion. Instead of sitting and talking like normal, it's one thing at a time. She sits. She places her lunch bag directly in front of her. She opens it. She takes her things out one by one: yogurt, spoon, napkin, carrots, nuts, water bottle.

"Your lunch looks a little, um, hamster-like?"

JennaLouise shakes her head fast. "What's happening here? With Elsie Jenkins? That last time she sat here shoveling mashed potatoes in her mouth wasn't just some one-time event?"

Why do I want to defend Elsie Jenkins? And from what exactly?

"Just be nice," I say. Because that's good advice. And should cover everything.

She makes an annoyed face and shrugs. Part of me wants to say that if she thought about it for even a second, JennaLouise would have to admit that *she* was the one who set this whole Elsie-Jenkins-in-my-life thing in motion when she said I'd go over to Elsie Jenkins's house. But I shouldn't even have to explain. It's not any kind of big deal to let someone sit with us at our table. It doesn't change anything.

I start to unpack my lunch. Bagel. I forgot; that's my whole lunch. I woke up late and barely had time to throw a hard bagel in my bag. It's better than buying lunch though.

And proof of that very fact shows up on Elsie Jenkins's tray. Meatball sub, some mix of peas and carrots and corn, and—this is alarming—only the corn is the right color. An apple, with at least three brown spots.

"That looks special," JennaLouise says.

"Yeah," Elsie Jenkins says, sitting right across from me. "The Clay Coves Intermediate School cafeteria meatball sub is surprisingly good."

"Really?" I say.

"That's a little hard to believe," JennaLouise says with a tiny bit of white yogurt on her spoon, paused on its way up to her mouth.

"Wanna taste?" Elsie Jenkins asks, holding out the sub.

"*No!*" JennaLouise says.

"Thanks anyway, though," I say, like some kind of mother.

"JennaLouise," Elsie Jenkins says. "Army and I are doing the beach cleanup Sunday morning."

"The two of you?" JennaLouise is not even trying to disguise the surprise in her face. Surprise, and is that disgust or just disbelief?

"You're welcome to join us," Elsie Jenkins says. "You get credit for community service." And then she gets down to the serious business of eating. She sporks up some miscolored vegetables and I look away.

I think about her surfing father, the big ring she wears around her neck, close to her heart, all that she has left of her father, and even though I never actually agreed to do the beach cleanup with her, I know I can't say no.

"I'm busy," JennaLouise says, and the tone of her voice makes me wonder if her feelings are hurt.

It seems like piece by piece, everything is slipping from what used to be normal.

The rest of lunch is awkward and kind of awful. Jenna-Louise eats in quiet slow motion. Elsie Jenkins is only interested in talking about the importance of cleaning beaches. And I have no appetite at all.

CHAPTER TWENTY

When I wake Sunday morning, all I can think is, *How do I get out of this? I cannot spend the morning cleaning a beach with Elsie Jenkins.* But as I hide under the covers, I know Elsie Jenkins will not allow me to blow this off. If I don't show up, she'll come to my house with a rope and haul me to the beach. Elsie Jenkins is persistent.

So I get up and pull on a pair of leggings, two shirts, and a windbreaker. And big old rubber boots.

Eating a bowl of Cheerios at the kitchen table, I remind my parents that I need a ride.

"Is that what you're wearing?" my mother asks.

I'm pretty sure the answer is obvious, as the clothes are on me. "Yeah," I say. "I thought the windbreaker would be good at the beach."

Mom takes the empty box of Cheerios from the table and folds it flat. She puts it in the recycling container. "So you and that girl, the vet's daughter, you're spending more time together?"

"Yeah," I say. It's hard to explain that it doesn't feel

voluntary. I expect her to continue her line of questioning but she's distracted by my clothes.

"You're sure you'll be warm enough in that?" she asks. "It's getting chilly."

"Finally," Dad says, walking through the kitchen. "Summer's finally over."

After we drop Navy at the soccer field, the drive to the beach is anything but quiet. My parents can't resist reminding me of the obvious fact that they consider themselves expert at all things cleanup.

"Did you pack rubber gloves?" Mom asks. "You probably didn't even think to pack gloves."

"They provide gloves," I say, not sure if it's true. Anyway, do you really need gloves to pick up old soda cans and . . . actually, thinking about some of the gross things I've seen at the beach, yeah, you definitely need gloves.

"What about a metal grabber? Will they give you one of those? And you'll obviously need trash bags," Mom says.

Dad has the radio on the news, listening to the weather, as always.

We pass the smoke-damage house Mom and Dad are working on and turn into the parking lot for the beach. There's a small blue tent set up with a big sign flapping in the wind that says SAVE OUR BEACHES. I say goodbye to my parents, get out of the car, and head over.

"Are you registered?" a man asks as I approach the biggest table.

"I have to be registered?" I ask, ready to run after the car.

"Oh, she's with me." Elsie Jenkins steps out from behind the next table. "Her name's right there." She points at a long list.

I smile and say, "Yes. I am registered."

Elsie Jenkins leads me to a row of plastic bins holding trash bags, and a table with a big cardboard box of disposable gloves. Of course! They *do* provide them.

It's not as cold as I thought it might be, but I can still feel the wind through all my layers. "Are there instructions?" I ask.

"Yeah," Elsie Jenkins says. "If you see something that's garbage, pick it up. If you see something that belongs on a beach, leave it."

"Ah," I say. "You are so wise, Elsie Jenkins."

She nods happily. "I really am."

We step onto the beach, sinking into the sand, which feels wrong and weird through these big old boots. "So we just look for garbage?"

"That's pretty much what a cleanup day is all about," she says.

There are a lot of people walking up and down the beach, white plastic bags whipping in the wind. We walk down to the tide line, where the wet sand makes rubber-boot-walking easier, and we head north, looking down.

"It's great that you felt up to doing this today," Elsie Jenkins says, reaching down to pick up a McDonald's wrapper.

Like Elsie Jenkins gives people a choice. Like there was any way on this earth I could not be here.

And then she says, "You probably know there are stages to, well, grief—to getting over a hard loss."

"Listen," I start, a warning very clear in my voice. But she doesn't. And I am not surprised.

"You'll feel so many different ways. You'll feel sad. You'll feel mad—"

"Elsie Jenkins, did you learn this on *Sesame Street*?" I reach down for a black plastic comb missing four teeth, and beneath it, a small piece of green sea glass. Comb into the trash bag, sea glass into my windbreaker pocket.

She stops walking. "No, from my mom. We talked a lot about this when my father died."

Oh my God. Her dad. What is wrong with me? "I'm sorry. I didn't mean to be rude."

I wonder if she comes to the beach all year long, like my dad and I do, or if that's something she only did with her dad. Did she bring up that grief thing to remind me that what I'm going through is nothing compared to what she's had to live through? That losing a dad is way greater than losing a dog?

I reach down to pick up a worn blue marble, drop it in my pocket. We walk together in silence for a while, and I pick up a Snickers wrapper, a used Band-Aid—I am so grateful for my gloves! I hurl the trash as quickly as possible into the bag.

"I handed in that form," she says. I had forgotten all about it. "For the assembly, for Service with a Wag. They gave me the petition sheet—if we both collect twenty-five signatures, we can submit our request to the PTA." She's like a little businesswoman. "Here." She reaches in her pocket and pulls out a folded piece of paper. "Can you start getting signatures so we can hand it in soon?"

"Okay," I say, shoving it in my pants pocket. I stop walking, hold still, and look out at the water, endless blue gray. Low waves, calm today, which makes the ocean seem somehow larger. I breathe slowly and look out at the spot where water and sky meet. It would be hard to feel anything other than peace when you look at that.

"Whatcha thinking about?" Elsie Jenkins asks.

That girl sure knows how to make me uncomfortable. "Nothing," I say.

"Uh-huh," she says. "Maybe I can help."

"With what? Look. My bag's halfway filled." I open it up to show her. "Well, a quarter filled, and it's not like I'm not *looking* for garbage, there just isn't that much to pick up!"

"Have you thought about getting another dog?"

It's like she's thrown me down on the ground and let off a series of kicks to the gut. Kick kick kick kick kick.

"My mom says lots of people put off getting a new dog, but as soon as they get one they wish they hadn't waited so long and I'm really only trying to help because you seem sad all the time and there are so many dogs that need homes and if you don't feel like you can get your own dog yet then you could foster a puppy or something. I really think—"

How can I escape?

She stands there staring at me. I know she's not going to give up. I look down at the sand and think of how Navy and I used to bury each other. I would like to quick-bury myself in the sand and let this moment pass. Or run to the lifeguard chair and hide behind it.

But no.

She stands there, waiting. Her right hand reaches up to her neck and she pulls out the ring and holds it gently.

I look back at the horizon line. When I was little, I dreamed of swimming all the way there and wondered what I'd find.

Elsie Jenkins is still staring at me.

I take a very deep breath and hold it. Then I say, "I wasn't thinking about my dog and I definitely don't want to talk about it." I feel like running back toward the parking lot, but it's not like I have a ride waiting for me.

I get very busy, focused on trash collection. I walk faster, farther from the water, and grab a driftwood stick to poke at piles of stuff that may or may not be hiding trash. Mussel shells, it turns out, can hide the plastic from six-packs and an empty suntan-lotion bottle. Even through the glove, the driftwood's roughness feels like it's leaving splinters in my hands.

I survive the long morning. But Elsie Jenkins is *so* persistent that when we say goodbye, as I climb into my dad's truck, she whispers into my ear, "Just *think* about fostering a puppy."

But no. I refuse to think about that.

CHAPTER TWENTY-ONE

When I get home from the beach all I want to do is collapse.

Navy's in the kitchen, telling Mom that he wants to ride his bike to his friend Grayson's house. I know where this is going. Navy's not allowed to ride alone yet. Which means I have to ride my bike with him to Grayson's place. My parents don't think there's a single thing unfair about it. But since he did a really nice thing for me with that box of Maybe's stuff, I don't complain. At least not out loud.

I'm trying to keep up—when did Navy get so fast?

At the end of Marigold Street, Mr. Sherman, who used to be principal at our elementary school, is approaching a parked car. There's something about the way he's walking that's odd—like he doesn't want to scare the people inside. When he gets to the car, he motions for the woman on the passenger side to roll down her window.

I stop riding and see that Navy has too. We walk our bikes up closer, in a nosy spying way, and hear Mr. Sherman ask, "Are you looking for the Clay Coves Inn by any chance?"

The woman looks at Mr. Sherman, seeming confused and grateful at the same time. "We've been driving around for more than a half hour and the GPS really wants us to believe this is where we're going and no offense, but your house, if that's your house, doesn't look like the Clay Coves Inn."

"Same address, different town," Mr. Sherman says. "For reasons no one may ever know, the Clay Coves Inn is not in Clay Coves. It's in Redbury. Here," he says, handing the woman something, and then he notices us. Snoopy us.

"Hello there, Army. Navy. Nice day for a ride." He smiles and then turns back to the woman in the car. "These directions will get you there. Or you can reprogram your GPS. Just make sure to say Redbury instead of Clay Coves."

The man who was driving leans over the woman and says, "But how did you—"

"You wouldn't believe how often this happens," Mr. Sherman says. "I started printing up directions years ago. It's easier than moving!"

Before he's all the way done with the couple in the car, I motion to Navy to get going, so maybe our nosiness won't be so obvious. I push away and start pedaling, imagining people ringing Mr. Sherman's bell, suitcases in hand, looking to check into his not-very-large house as though it really were the Clay Coves Inn. There's something so . . . accepting about it. A lot of people would turn out the lights and not answer when the doorbell rang, like the Elliots, who put a note on their door every single Halloween about why they're away. It's been two weddings, one funeral, a family emergency, and a bar mitzvah. Sure. All on Halloween.

After I drop Navy off at Grayson's and tell him I'll be back in a couple of hours, I decide to take the long way home, past Clay Coves Elementary. I pull my sweatshirt hood up over my helmet—the cold air's making my ears hurt, reminding me of everything I hate about winter.

There are scribbled black-hatted witches and orange jack-o'-lanterns taped up in the windows. Isn't that one of the greatest things about life in elementary school, how every month, practically, has a coloring assignment? Colored leaves, jack-o'-lanterns, turkeys, Pilgrims, Christmas trees, menorahs, Martin Luther King Jr.'s face, hearts, four-leaf clovers, bunnies, and smiling suns. Every year, the same pictures, colored almost the same way go up on the same classroom windows, facing out so everyone passing by can see.

It's only been a couple of years since I was part of that—coloring famous faces and animals and plants and shapes. I didn't think of it as simple and comforting then, just like I didn't know how lucky I was every day that Maybe was alive. I can't stand the memories of the times I was impatient with him—rushing his walks when it was cold or rainy. Or the way I made him leave the room when he tried to eat my water bottle when I was trying to do homework. There were a million things I did wrong instead of just enjoying every single minute of his life.

At the side of the school, there's one car in the parking lot. Irene's car, I think.

I ride slowly over and leave my bike by the fence. Madison's sitting on a spot that isn't supposed to be climbed to—just this little roof on the playground structure—something that's there for decoration, about eight feet off the ground. How did she get up there? There's a ladder to the platform where kids get on the slide but she's sitting on the green roof above that.

Irene's sitting on the bench with Schuyler in her lap. Or maybe Tyler. The other baby is sleeping, his face smushed against one side of the double stroller.

"Hi," I say. "I thought that was your car."

Irene smiles at me and then looks at Madison, still smiling. "She can climb anything."

I could never—literally, not ever—climb to where Madison is. I couldn't even make it across the elementary school playground's monkey bars. Not then. Not now. Weak arms, and not interested enough to work at it until I could do it.

I watch Madison. The way she holds her head makes me think there's something about being *up* that Madison really needs. I wonder if it makes her feel something like the way I feel under all those blankets—safer? Away from all the noise and mess and activity and worry of home. Is that what Madison feels when she sits high above the world, looking out? I think so—I hope so.

"She is an incredible climber," I say. I've been feeling so

sad that she can't tell people what she wants or needs. But looking at her up there, I realize that even without words, she finds a way. "Better there than your roof, right?"

Irene does something to remind me, in a hurry, why I'm not supposed to stick my nose in other people's business: she bursts into tears. This grown-up woman puts her hand over her mouth and sort of gasp-sobs and then stands, handing off Schuyler or Tyler into my arms. Then she walks a few steps away.

What am I supposed to do? Sit with this baby? Make sure Irene's okay? Apologize?

Madison seems okay—better than okay—where she is. The stroller baby's still sleeping. So I ask the baby in my arms if he'd like to go on the baby swings. He doesn't answer. As I carry him over to the swings, I can't help but wonder if some of his massive weight has to do with the droopy diaper he's wearing. Ew.

"Should I push you?"

The baby, although this may very well be by accident, points in front of him. I take that as a yes.

"You got it."

And that's all I do. I push the baby gently on the bucket baby swing. And keep an eye on Madison. And sneak glances over at Irene.

The trees behind the school are always the first to let go of their leaves. They're completely bare and there are giant mounds of crunchy-looking brown leaves piled up near the parking lot. Irene moves closer to us and leans against the swing set.

"Are you okay?"

"I'm fine," Irene says. "I'm so sorry, Army."

"No. Don't be sorry."

I think and push the swing. And think and think. I can't come up with a question that does *not* involve poking my nose where it doesn't belong, but I feel like I need to know and so I ask it anyway. "Is Madison able to tell you what she needs?"

Irene nods yes before she starts talking. "Sometimes. She surprises me all the time. Two weeks ago, I realized she makes a *ch ch ch* noise in the car when she wants me to turn. I think she's imitating the turn signal. It's how we ended up here today—I was just taking a drive to get the boys to sleep. And she has a way of understanding directions, of almost shutting out everything else to get from point A to point B."

Like the way she walked so confidently down the middle of the street, turned into her driveway, and climbed in the window of her new house.

"Does she go to school?" I ask. I can't really imagine how a kid who doesn't talk learns in a classroom.

"I'd been homeschooling her because the school where we lived wasn't right for her. We were doing okay. But it feels like we've been slipping. It's time to get her into the school here. The program's supposed to be pretty good. And I have all the paperwork, but it's all a little . . . overwhelming. When we moved here for this new job, Kyle was told he wouldn't have to travel for the first six months. But his supervisor quit right before he started and he had to do more than he'd signed up for . . . it's been too much."

Irene walks a few steps to the bench, kicking up some dry brown leaves as she goes. Big clouds move in front of the sun.

"But Madison going on the roof, running away—it's so dangerous. When I think of all the things that could happen when she gets out of the house—the swimming pools, the cars in the street, strangers. . . . We've decided to try the alarms on the phones."

I give the swing another push and join Irene on the bench.

"Before we lived here we got her a tracking device but she couldn't stand the feel of it and kept ripping it off until she broke it. Of course she did. It was keeping her from doing what she needs to do to feel better. I feel like I do the best I can to let Madison be who she is while keeping her safe. But there are people—lots of them—who would tell you I should try to keep Madison from repeating certain behaviors. It just seems cruel to me, though, to keep her from doing what she needs to do to feel better. It's a very strange and hard-to-see line between what Madison needs and what the world says is okay."

Then Irene goes silent. I can't blame her. It sounds like

all of that could crush a person. She turns and looks at me. "Oh, Army, why am I dumping all this on you?"

"It's okay." I can't think of anything else to say.

"I try to have faith. I do. But it's so hard. I've reached out to some people online, people who live in this county and have autistic children. But with the twins and Madison, it's hard to get out of the house to go to one of their meet-ups. And we just can't afford to hire some extra help. Right here, right now, you're watching us have the most normal day we've had since we moved here." She looks around the playground. "We hardly go out at all because so many things upset her—a noisy truck, a bad smell, sometimes it seems like nothing causes it."

I've never had a conversation like this. Part of me wonders if Irene realizes I'm only twelve.

I walk to the swing, which has barely any back-and-forth left to it. The baby bangs on the safety seat. "I'll push him," Irene says. And she does for a while. She isn't talking anymore.

So I walk over to Madison.

Madison is an absolute and total mystery, but something tells me that standing nearby, being with her, near her, is the right thing to do. It's what I want and I hope I'm not wrong in thinking that it's what Madison wants too. She's not looking at me but she knows I'm here. "You look happy," I say. Or maybe it's content, but I don't know if she'd know that word. Or the word *happy*.

It's a very helpless feeling, knowing this family needs help but not being able to do anything about it.

Right now, though, Madison doesn't look like she needs any help at all. Up above, she sits, still, leaning her face into the wind.

CHAPTER TWENTY-TWO

On Monday, Dad was the only one talking about a storm that was hitting Jamaica and Cuba. By Tuesday, weather reports were mentioning the possibility of the hurricane heading our way. And now, even though the weekend is a few days away and storm paths can change, everyone's convinced there's going to be a huge storm here along the New Jersey coast on Saturday night. The newscasters have started calling it Frankenstorm.

It's impossible to completely ignore all the storm-of-the-century hype, but you could safely say I'm not exactly worrying about it. It'll probably end up being just a regular rainstorm. Looking out my bedroom window Wednesday after school—barely a breeze, sun shining—it's impossible to believe anything resembling danger is coming.

But the over-the-top warnings have been great for business! Mom and Dad are hardly ever home, out finishing up jobs, helping people who've been hit hard in the past to prepare for this storm, and delivering hurricane boxes. They've missed dinner the last two nights. Navy and I are on a first-name basis with the pizza delivery guy (Hubert!).

They've delivered the fifty hurricane boxes we had on hand, but they keep getting more calls, from clients they've worked with in the past and new people.

Mom and Dad keep a ton of supplies in our storage space, so even when the shelves in local stores are emptied, they have everything they need to make new boxes.

But all this time out driving to clients' houses means they've had no time at all to make their hurricane warning calls. Even after they've delivered a box, Dad likes to leave a message reminding clients what precautions they need to take. He says it's important for customer service. But now that there's an actual storm coming, or at least in the forecast, neither of them has time to make all the calls. They're reaching some people on their cells when they're grabbing food or getting gas, but they still have a ton more to do.

Navy keeps insisting he should be allowed to make the calls, but my parents say clients won't feel calmed down by hearing a little kid's voice reminding them about hurricane safety. They're not wrong.

I sit down at my computer with a bowl of baby carrots and though my brain is pretending it has no idea what is about to happen, my fingers don't hesitate. Not that I'm ready. Not that I'm looking. Not that what Elsie Jenkins said at the beach last weekend opened a tiny door in my heart. I type the search words: *foster puppy, Clay Coves, NJ.*

The results page: SPCA, of course. I take one look and realize I'm not even close to ready for pictures of puppies with pleading eyes.

I'm about to shut it down when something at the bottom of the page gets my attention—Service with a Wag. Those amazing dogs from Navy's Cub Scouts meeting!

I click through to the page and come to a screen that says: *Our mission at Service with a Wag is to improve the quality of life for people with disabilities with our trained assistance dogs.*

I read on. My head starts buzzing. Service with a Wag doesn't only train dogs for people who can't see and people who have seizures. They also train dogs to get help when someone is in danger. To carry medicine in a special backpack and answer the door by pulling a lever. There's a whole section about service dogs for autistic kids. And that section instantly becomes the most addictive thing that has ever been on the Internet (with the possible exception of baby-goats-in-pajamas videos). I read stories about kid after kid whose life was completely changed by a service dog.

But what makes me almost stop breathing is this:

Sawyer is a six-year-old boy who wanders. But now that he has Scout, everything is different. One time Sawyer got away when visiting his grandmother in another state. Scout tracked Sawyer right down. Scout can also wear a GPS and be tethered to Sawyer so if Sawyer darts off out of his parents' sight they can find him. Scout keeps Sawyer safe.

That right there is magic.

I'm bouncing in my seat, up and down like a twitchy little kid. Like I found buried treasure, like I won the lottery, like I maybe just discovered the very thing that could actually help. I want everything at once, but what I want most of all is to let Irene know that there might be a life-changing solution. Madison needs a magic dog!

I can't even wait, can't take time to think. I grab a sweatshirt and start to head out of the room when I remember one thing. The price. I have no idea what it costs.

So I go back to the computer and there, oh. There it is. Oh God.

Eighteen. Thousand. Dollars.

I have just over $400 in my bank account, saved up from birthdays and grandparents and stuff. How am I going to get $18,000? How could anything that's not a car or a house cost so much money? If they can't afford to hire help, I don't think there's a chance Madison's parents have that kind of money.

Okay, but there's a page of fundraising ideas, with lots of different suggestions. And that makes me think of Jenna-Louise's mom. This is what she does. It's her job. I bet she'd help me.

But as I read on, a bad feeling settles in. There's the cost. There's also the fact that it'll take eighteen months from the time they apply to the time they can get a dog, at the very soonest. The wait is usually even longer than that. That seems like way too long. So much could go wrong between now and then.

CHAPTER TWENTY-THREE

I don't know how to define this relationship with Elsie Jenkins, but if we are friends, then (a) that's a surprise—how did that even happen? And (b) I really ought to give her some advice about how friends interact. She is the texting sergeant of friendship. *Do this! Meet me here! Prepare!*

My experience with friends is pretty much JennaLouise. Everything with us has always been natural and easy. But the last few days, things with JennaLouise have felt a little off-kilter, maybe because Elsie Jenkins keeps sitting at our table. And today, when everyone was overreacting to the possibility of a hurricane tomorrow, and Elsie Jenkins seemed to agree with me that weather forecasters hardly ever get it right, JennaLouise looked bored and had nothing to say on the subject.

I am thinking about this after school when I get a text from Elsie Jenkins saying:

WILL BE IN FRONT OF YOUR HOUSE IN 12 MINUTES.

I wait on the front steps—not sure if I'm looking for a car or a bike. It might not surprise me if Elsie Jenkins parachuted in.

Mmm. It's so warm again. What a weird fall. Some trees are still refusing to let go all the way—holding on to most of their leaves. But the sugar maples on the other side of the street have lost most of them, piles of leaves along the curb, waiting for the truck with its Snuffleupagus trunk to come by and slurp them all up. I hope for the little kids that it stays warm for a while. There's nothing worse than a freezing Halloween. Except a rainy one.

It makes me think of the year JennaLouise and I went as a two-headed Pippi Longstocking. I text her:

Remember two-headed Pippi Longstocking?

She responds:

Why didn't anyone recognize us? The sticking up braids made it pretty clear. And the freckles.

To which I answer:

Because we are misunderstood.
But perfect.

And I feel a little better about the state of us.

"Can you come with me?" Elsie Jenkins yells out when

she's still three houses away. She's walking with big bags over each shoulder. "I'm going to deliver some stuff for my mom."

"Okay," I say. "Where are we going?"

"You know Linda and Sue, right? They needed medicine and formula and stuff for some kittens and my mom asked me to deliver it."

"I was there the day they got the kittens," I say. "Johnny on the Spot found them."

"Johnny who?"

"That guy who drives an old pickup truck and gathers up people's garbage. I'm sure you've seen him—he's always out."

"You mean Mr. Elkton? In the white truck?"

My face grows hot. I've never heard anyone call him anything other than Johnny on the Spot. I never stopped to think that he probably had a real name.

"He's brought a lot of hurt animals to my mom."

Those bags on her shoulders look heavy. "Want me to carry one of those?"

"I thought you'd never ask," she says.

I thought you never waited for someone to ask, I think but don't say as I lean over and grab a bag and slide the handles to my shoulder. "What is all this stuff?"

"Supplies for some kittens. There's this special stuff, KMR—kitten milk replacer—that's for kittens whose mother isn't around."

We walk up the front steps of Linda and Sue's house and ring the bell.

Linda opens the door and says, "Elsie. You have the KMR and meds? That's great. Thank your mom for me. Oh, Army. You guys are friends? Nice! But Army, how are you not out with your parents? Your dad said they've been crazy busy with that storm coming."

"If it comes," I say.

"Let's hope it doesn't," she says, looking up at the sky. "Hey, Army—you were here the day we got this litter, right? Do you guys want to come in and see how they're doing?"

Elsie Jenkins nods and steps into the house.

Linda is about to turn and follow her, but then she stops and faces me. "Are you doing any better?" she asks, looking me in the eye. "I miss seeing you and Maybe together."

I swallow. "I miss him so much," I whisper. She pulls me into a hug and I have to work hard to not cry. I think she expects me to say more, but I've already said a lot. Five words, but five really hard words.

"Let me show you these little monsters," she says, letting go gently.

I follow her and Elsie Jenkins downstairs to the basement. Linda turns on the lights and it's like an abandoned small zoo or pet shop or something. Everything is animal stuff. Over in the corner, there's a cardboard box with a towel over it and something like a heating lamp next to it. There's also a space heater blowing—it's hot down here!

When Linda lifts the towel, there are the kittens, in what looks like a nest. Two are sleeping but the other three are wiggling and squirming. They're still tiny, though possibly a little longer than they were that first day. Could they really grow in just a week and a half?

"Hungry again," Linda says. "It's a good thing I don't have anything else I need to do since I spend my whole life feeding these guys."

It makes me want to ask what Linda does, but I don't think she has a job. I see Sue coming home in the evening lots of days, but Linda seems to be home almost all the time.

"Want some help?" Elsie Jenkins asks.

Linda smiles and sighs like Elsie Jenkins offered to be her cheerful servant for a year.

"Show us what to do," I say.

I figured we'd dump some food in a bowl and watch to make sure the kittens didn't choke. Instead, it's more like being a chemist—we watch Linda measure out powdered KMR and water in a little bottle. She shakes it and adds medicine and then uses a syringe to feed one of the tiny kittens. "You have to be careful," Linda says. "Don't give them more than they can take. It's better to let them suck it out than to squeeze it in. Like this."

I look at Linda and the kitten and realize that there's a whole lot of magic down here. Also a lot of supplies and hard work that go into making that kind of magic.

How many houses in my neighborhood are hiding secrets like this? Does every front door have a different kind of unexpected magic behind it? Johnny—I mean Mr. Elkton must have a house filled with things his neighbors threw away—what does he do with all of it? And Mrs. Rooney transformed balls of wool into mittens.

I cannot take my eyes off the kitten Linda is holding—it's so cute! I wouldn't mind spending the rest of my life feeding tiny kittens.

"I'll finish up Finlay here," she says. "Do you guys want to each take one of the gray ones and just load—actually, here, Elsie. Hold Finlay for a sec."

"They all have names?" I ask.

"You'd think so. But no. Just Finlay. Sue won't let me name the rest of them until we're sure they'll all live, and since Finlay's the biggest and healthiest, well, she has the best shot." She hands Finlay to Elsie Jenkins and reaches for another.

"Here, you take this mush ball, hold her like this, against you, to keep her warm."

She hands me a tiny bit of silvery-gray fur and I bring the unnamed kitten over to a chair in the corner and sit, pulling it close against me. Linda gives me a syringe, but when I hold it, the kitten just lies there, so I move the syringe closer to her mouth. She pokes with her nose a little before opening her mouth. And then she starts to drink. Success!

She's so tiny. It's a miracle she can even open that mouth enough to take in liquid. But she seems to be getting it now, so I have a chance to look around some more. This is the strangest room—crates, glass cages, a big old-fashioned white wire birdcage. Clothes are piled on the floor next to a washing machine. It smells a little, and the superwarm air down here isn't helping that at all.

Wait. What's—the kitten is shaking. Then she stops. And starts again. What was I thinking, trusting myself with a tiny baby animal, one that might not even survive losing its mama? The kitten keeps shaking. Or quaking. Like a spasm. Is this a seizure? I am struck dumb and silent by fear and Linda and Elsie Jenkins aren't looking at me. Linda's getting the third kitten set up for feeding and I can't get my stupid mouth working, and the kitten keeps spazzing out and finally I'm able to say, "Something's wrong! Something's happening!"

Linda calmly turns. She looks at the kitten. She looks at me. It feels as though it takes three hours. She smiles! And then she says, "Hiccups. That one always gets the hiccups. I should have warned you. She eats too fast. My bad. No worries."

It takes a while but I start to breathe regularly. And when the gray kitten has finished eating, I carefully place her back in the warm nest and pick up an orange one, hold it tight, wait for a full syringe from Linda, and then let the kitten drink its lunch. Or whatever this is.

I get a text.

Hey! Margaret Ann said she could drop me off. You free?

And I write back.

At neighbor's house with Elsie Jenkins. Home soon.

"I'm going to spare you the bathrooming portion of our day," Linda says. "But if you ever want to learn that, please know I'd be happy to show you."

"They don't just go in a litter box?" I ask.

Linda laughs. "Soon, but no, not yet. It involves washcloths and it's not pretty and I think we'll just leave it at that."

And so we do.

"Thank you so much," Linda says.

"Anytime," I say. It's a good feeling to leave the animals, knowing their bellies are full and they'll be warm and comfortable in their nest. I hope the other four end up with beautiful, perfect names.

CHAPTER TWENTY-FOUR

We're standing in front of my house and Elsie Jenkins seems to grow roots. Her tan sneakers are planted solidly on the first step up onto the porch, unmoving. I thought she'd say goodbye and head home. Nothing. Finally, I ask, "Do you want to come in?" despite the fact that the question is completely unnecessary. Elsie Jenkins *is* coming in.

At the sound of a door opening, my mother calls out, "Army? I need the Armed Forces' help to get every—" She stops talking when she walks into the hallway and sees I'm not alone. "Oh, hello?"

The question in her voice makes me laugh. "Mom, this is Elsie Jenkins. Elsie Jenkins, this is my mom."

"Hi, Mrs. Morand," Elsie Jenkins says, her hand out for a shake. Where exactly did this adult-type girl come from?

Mom shakes her hand, looking kind of impressed. "Are you girls hungry?"

I can imagine the food she has in mind. Brown juice. Beans.

"No," I say. "Thanks. We were just going to my room for a little while."

Mom holds up her hand like a traffic cop. "We got twenty-two calls today from new customers desperate for boxes. Dad picked up everything we had left from the storage place, so I want to make sure we have what we need for those and for anyone else who may call. I need you to do inventory of everything that's now in the basement while I make hurricane calls. I may need to go to the store, so let me know if we need anything. I hope we're all set. Who knows if anything's left at the store."

"I'm in," Elsie Jenkins says.

Not that she was asked.

Not that that should be surprising.

My instinct is to protest—why should I have to do work when I have a friend over?

But I also know on some level that when I'm with Elsie Jenkins it's better to have something to do, to focus on, like a beach cleanup or feeding kittens. The kind of comfortable, mindless conversation JennaLouise and I always have doesn't happen with Elsie Jenkins. But still, there's something new and surprising about being friends with her. Or whatever this is.

"Where do we start?" Elsie Jenkins asks.

"I like this one," Mom says. "Let's keep her."

"Oh, JennaLouise might be coming over," I tell my

mom. I check my phone but there's nothing new. Just my mention of Elsie Jenkins in my last text. And then silence.

It's embarrassing bringing someone into our gross basement. It's not unlike Linda's basement in a way, except that there's nothing magic about this. Mom and Dad have cleared out an area and filled it with the supplies for hurricane boxes—the boxes themselves and all the things we fill them with and the packing tape that holds the boxes together. And packed even tighter against the walls is all the equipment for Never Happened that can't fit in the garage.

I open the top drawer of the filing cabinet and right in front, where it belongs, is a small stack of copies of the printed list of a hurricane box's contents, where I can record how many we have of each item that goes into a box. I take one copy out and attach it to the clipboard that's also right where it belongs—hanging off a hook on the side of the cabinet.

"Sorry about this, Elsie Jenkins."

"Why do you do that?" she asks, starting to count the plastic-wrapped folded blankets stacked on the basement floor.

"Well, I'm sure this isn't what you had in mind when you came over," I say. "Taking inventory." Though to be honest, I'm quite sure I'd never be able to guess what Elsie has in mind, ever. "So I'm sorry we put you to work."

"I actually like being useful," she says. "I kind of look for ways to be useful." She taps the blanket at the top of the pile and says, "Twenty-nine. There are twenty-nine blankets."

I write that on the inventory sheet and start to count the battery packs.

"But that's not what I was talking about," she says. "Why do you and JennaLouise call me Elsie Jenkins? Instead of just Elsie?" She starts counting bags of trail mix. "Is it because of JennaLouise? Does a first name not seem like enough or something?"

"JennaLouise *is* her first name," I say. "JennaLouise-NoSpace."

"Just twelve bags of trail mix," Elsie Jenkins says. "Unless there's more somewhere that I'm not seeing."

Navy must have gotten into the trail mix again.

"So what's her middle name?" Elsie Jenkins asks.

"She doesn't have one. Let me finish counting these batteries. Give me a sec." I point but I'm really not counting. I'm trying to think of an answer. Because the real answer isn't that nice. JennaLouise and I have called Elsie Jenkins by both names since we met her. It's just who she is, the girl who always wears tan clothes. Who's usually pretty quiet except in class when she knows an answer and then you kind of wish she'd be quiet because she goes on and on and on. Are we being mean? Like the way referring to Marcus as the sniffer is mean, but seriously, that boy sniffs everything and it's impossible not to think of him that way. Can I squirm out of an answer? "Would you rather I just call you Elsie?"

Elsie Jenkins starts nodding before I even finish the

question. "Okay, Elsie. But I might mess up. I've been thinking of you as Elsie Jenkins for the past year. One more time on these battery packs." I count and write down the number fifty-nine. "Can I ask you a question?"

Elsie nods and says, "Forty-one first-aid kits."

I write it down. "No broken seals?"

She nods again.

"Why do you always wear tan?"

She reaches for her ring and after a few seconds says, "When my father died, for a long time, I was a mess. I put on clothes without noticing that I was wearing things that my mother thought clashed and for some reason that made her crazy. So whenever I outgrew something, she bought me new stuff and I don't even know if she noticed that everything she was buying was tan, but it worked in a way, because I could still get dressed without thinking, which was the best I could do then. And once everything was all tan, there were no clashing clothes to set off my mom. I think she saw that—purple and green together, or whatever—as a reminder of losing my dad. And anyway, in the tan, I figured I blended in, which isn't the worst thing, you know?"

"Wow," I say. "Okay."

We get back to the business of counting.

"I have one more question," I say. "Why did you suddenly want to be my friend?" It might be a little rude to ask your average person that, but I think it's exactly the kind of question Elsie'd ask. Also, she is not your average person.

"You won't like it," Elsie says. "But I'm always honest and if you want to know I'll tell you."

"Tell me."

"It had to do with what happened to your dog. My mom knew. Well. I mean, she knew it broke your heart. And she said to be a good friend to you."

"Your mother made you be friends with me?" I don't even pretend to count anything.

"No—I mean—well, I see how you could think that. But I think she really was doing it more for me than for you. I don't know if you've noticed, but I don't have a ton of friends. And my mom knows I like helping people and I think she knew you were a good person, so she pushed me toward you in a way because you were a good person going through a bad time."

"Okay," I say. And I think about the picture of Maybe up in my room that I swiped from the Jenkinses' house. I should give it back. Or maybe just return it when no one's looking. After I make a copy for myself.

I open a box of candles and count them out so we can divide them up for the remaining boxes. "Did you come up with a whole plan? First I'll talk to Army about that Cub Scout presentation and then I'll invite her to the beach cleanup? Like, did you have a whole be-friends-with-Army checklist?"

Elsie shakes her head. "Nothing like that. You can't plan everything in advance. I just try to move in the right direction and hope it all works out. It usually does. But now that you mention it, have you gotten the signatures on the petition?"

I have not. The petition has only my signature. I need to do better. "I will," I say.

I look around. Elsie Jenkins—Elsie—gets things done. It's been so much easier doing this with her help. It makes me think about how impossible it is to even know where to begin, to turn the great idea of getting Madison a magic dog into something I can actually start to do.

I haven't had anyone I could talk about it with. Talking to JennaLouise about Madison's family made me feel squirmy. My mom thinks Madison's home is a dangerous place I should avoid. Elsie said she likes being useful. So while we finish taking inventory, I tell her everything—all about Madison and how a service dog could change their lives but they cost so much and there are fundraising suggestions, but can I even start on that before I tell Irene, but I can't say anything to Irene until I'm sure I can get them a dog because could you imagine getting their hopes up and then not being able to pull it off? "So it's like a circle," I say. "And I can't start because I don't know what to do first."

"You don't have to know everything up front," Elsie says.

That would be a relief if it's true.

"Army," Mom calls. "Are you two done yet?"

"Just finished," I yell back. "You'll need to get more trail mix."

"I could help," Elsie says.

"You already have," I say.

CHAPTER TWENTY-FIVE

I've been in stores the days before Christmas and at the grocery store the morning of Thanksgiving when Mom forgot to get yams. But busy? *This*, helping my parents with their work stuff the day of the storm, or at least the storm that's in the forecast, is busy.

There have been hurricanes before, of course, but it seems like the news and the government and everyone all over New Jersey thinks this is going to be a big one. I seem to be the only person who remembers that they've said that before. Many times. Though I couldn't be my parents' daughter without knowing that you need to prepare as though it's going to be bad no matter what.

My parents are out delivering the boxes we made last night. I'm making more for the last orders we received this morning, and Navy is on phone duty. Mom didn't finish making the hurricane calls, so Dad recorded a message and Navy got half of his wish—he's dialing the numbers and playing the recording.

So the background music to my box making is my father's

voice, repeating: "Hello, this is Never Happened calling to help ensure your hurricane safety. If you have ordered and not yet received a hurricane box, it will be delivered before day's end. Be sure to secure or bring inside anything that can be picked up by the wind. Turn refrigerators and freezers to highest setting to prepare for a power outage. Turn off propane tanks. Charge cell phones. Fill your bathtubs with water for toilets. Fill your cars with gas. If you have a generator, make sure you have the diesel fuel needed to run it as well as enough food and water for all humans and animals in your home. Have cash on hand. Be smart and be safe."

And then again.

I recite along with Dad under my breath. ". . . your cars with gas . . . make sure . . . cash on hand. Be smart and safe . . ."

I build a big cardboard box and tape and retape the bottom. Then I put the heavy/unbreakable stuff at the bottom—a small case of water, batteries, canned fruit, peanut butter, protein shakes, and a flashlight. The light things go up top—energy bars, cereal, rice cakes, trail mix, candles, a blanket. Then I seal the box with packing tape. And start again. When two are done, I stack them on the hand truck and wheel them to the garage, where Dad will get them for the last round of deliveries. I feel like a dark-and-stormy version of one of Santa's elves.

"Hey, Army!" Navy calls down. "My next call is Jenna-Louise's house!"

"Don't call them," I say, my brain pushing ahead past this storm to seeing if JennaLouise's mom can give me some ideas for community fundraising to help Madison's family get a magic dog.

"They're on the list!" Navy says.

"I know," I say. "I'll make that call."

"Okay," Navy says. And then, "So do you have like a hockey helmet or a puck or any zombie stuff?"

Navy can be so exhausting. "What are you talking about?"

"Halloween. Duh. My zombie hockey player costume?"

"No, Navy. I'm all out of zombie hockey player stuff." I feel mean, though. I remember how exciting Halloween was when I was his age, and it's less than a week away.

After I finish the last box, I stay in the basement for privacy and call JennaLouise's house.

"Why are you calling the house phone?" JennaLouise asks.

"And also hi, right?"

"Sure," JennaLouise says.

"Why didn't you come over yesterday?" I ask.

"You were already hanging out with a friend. Or an Elsie Jenkins. Whatever."

I don't want to fight with JennaLouise. I want to make a best-friends pledge to her because she always will be mine. So I just say the truth. "I miss you."

"Yeah," JennaLouise says. "I miss you too."

It's quiet for a while, and then Dad's voice starts up again upstairs, reminding me why I called. "I'm actually calling to talk to your mom. I have to do the whole 'Turn off propane tanks. Charge cell phones . . . Fill your cars with gas' speech."

"Don't your parents usually do that?" JennaLouise asks.

"They're both out and didn't finish the calls, so Navy and I are helping."

"Do you seriously want to talk to my mom?"

"Yeah."

"Well, better you than me. She's kind of cranky because an event just got canceled. Hang on a sec."

I wait until Daphne answers.

"Hey, honey. What's up?"

"Hurricane stuff," I say. "Gas. Propane tanks. Charge phones. Plenty of cash on hand. And also, can I ask you a question?"

"Of course!"

"When you do a fundraiser, to raise like a whole lot of money, how do you even know where to begin?"

"What do you mean?"

"It would take a long time to explain, but basically there's a family in my neighborhood that needs help. But it's going to take a lot of money, like a ton. So what would I do to, like, organize a fundraiser or something, the kind of thing you do? Where do I even begin, I—"

"I don't mean to cut you off, but I have a . . . I don't even know what." She pauses for a second. "Do you know what serendipity is?" She doesn't wait for an answer. "It's like a happy coincidence that was meant to happen. A client just canceled on me because of this Frankenstorm that probably won't even happen and they don't want to reschedule and don't seem to care that I have all these gift baskets for the silent auction and Army, my dear, you would be doing me an enormous favor if you would take it all off my hands and use it to help that family."

"But I don't have a plan or anything. I wouldn't even know what to do with all of your stuff, so I'm not sure—"

"I'll help you figure that all out, but for starters, you could think about getting a table at Clay Coves Community Day next month and holding a basket auction there—it doesn't have to be a whole big event, and since you're trying to raise the money for a neighbor, well, a community day seems like a good start. I'd be happy to help you. Really. You should have asked me already. But this is what *I* need. Can I bring this stuff to you now? It's all over my dining room and kitchen and it is making me nuts to look at it and I need it out of here as soon as possible and if you guys have the room I'll bring it right over."

I look at the basement wall where all the supplies for hurricane boxes had been piled—wide-open space.

Serendipity.

CHAPTER TWENTY-SIX

I hope it's possible to start with serendipity and build from there. Just go with it and make things happen before you totally understand how to do all of it. Kind of like what Elsie Jenkins—what Elsie said. Get moving in the right direction. I'm going to have all that stuff, Daphne's gift baskets. And Daphne will help. There's just the tiny issue of letting Irene know.

"Be right back, Navy," I call as I head out the door. I race over to Madison's house.

I ring the bell and Irene answers, looking exhausted. Her face falls when she sees me, and I realize I've only come over when Madison's been out. But when I don't deliver any bad news, she smiles and invites me in.

I step inside and it looks worse than ever—like an in-house storm has torn through, pulling things up in the air and dropping them down to the ground. Irene says, "Let me just—" and then she steps over a pile of laundry and out of the room and I can't hear her anymore.

"Say hi to Army, Tyler," Irene says, walking back, holding a baby. The baby smiles at me, which is kind of like saying hi. He's so cute. If they weren't smelly so often, I might really love babies.

In the middle of the room, Schuyler is sitting in a swing that's moving back and forth. He's passed out.

Madison is standing in the hall right next to the living room, her hands waving. At me, I think. I wave back.

Irene's looking at me, surely wondering why I stopped by. As though to save me the embarrassment of all that silence, she says, "Did I tell you what the twins are going to be for Halloween?"

I shake my head.

"Bumblebees."

I can't help but smile. Silence starts settling in again, so I find a tiny piece of courage and blurt it out. "Have you ever heard of service dogs? Like for Madison? They train these dogs to help autistic kids. There's this website I found and there's a group not far from here, I saw them at my brother's Cub Scout meeting, and—"

"Oh, Kyle's allergic to dogs, hon."

Kyle. The dad.

Is allergic.

To dogs.

Just like that.

Done.

No magic dog.

No magic answers.

I am so deeply stunned by disappointment that I just stand there.

Then I remember that luckily there's a hurricane in the forecast! "I'm here because I wanted to check in to see if you're all set for the big spooky storm that's supposed to come tonight. Is there anything you need?"

"Oh, that's right! Your family's in the storm business. Kyle went to the store a couple of days ago and picked up everything we need. But it's sweet of you to ask. Wait! You haven't met Kyle! Wait here." She leaves the room.

I will not burst into tears.

I so wanted to give this family some magic. Something that could change their lives. Something seriously helpful.

Irene comes back with a tall man with a very short haircut who's holding his hand out to me. We shake. It makes me feel like Elsie. "Nice to meet you." My voice is wobbly.

"I've heard a lot about you, Army. Thank you for all the help you've given Irene."

I can't keep looking at him. He has no idea what I had hoped to give them. But what I've done for them hasn't been anything, really. I wanted to change things, make it better for them.

I have to get out of here.

"Okay, so if you need anything, call us or come over or whatever, my parents have all the equipment in the world if this storm ever really happens. Bye, everyone." I walk to where Madison's still standing and raise my hand to wave again. "Bye, Madison." I can't be sure if she's looking at me because I'm looking down, holding in no-magic-dog tears.

CHAPTER TWENTY-SEVEN

Back home, Navy has finished the phone calls and is checking the batteries in all the flashlights. Dad texts to say it's still "all Armed Forces on deck"; I need to come along on the last round of deliveries so he can finish up faster. He'll pick me up in an hour so we can be done before the storm starts. Mom got one more delivery and once she gets back, she and Navy will stay home to get the house ready.

Daphne should be here soon with whatever she's dropping off. Oh God. Wait. I won't need to do a fundraiser if Madison can't have a magic dog—what would I even be fundraising for? What am I going to do with all of Daphne's stuff? But there's an idea scratching its way to the surface. Aunt Emily is allergic to dogs. And Aunt Emily has a dog, Strudel. He's a no-allergy dog. And she's not allergic to him. At all.

On the computer, I go back to Service with a Wag's site and do a search on the word *allergy*, but nothing comes up. When I look at the pictures on the photo page—so many pictures!—some of the dogs look like poodles. Like different-colored Strudels.

I read up on a few different sites about poodles. Most people allergic to dogs do not have that reaction to poodles, because poodles have hair, not fur. I don't really get what the difference is, but it sounds promising.

But wait. What's that at the bottom?

There's a link that says HELP US MAKE IT BETTER FOR A CHILD: FOSTER A PUPPY. There are pictures of adorable puppies—marshmallow-soft golden retrievers, melty-eyed black Labs, wavy-haired baby doodles. I accidentally look and look and look and it stretches my heart and tries to pull it completely apart. But my heart survives.

Service with a Wag needs people to provide foster homes for future assistance dogs. That's what it says. To train them and socialize them and return to SWAW every two months for checkups. At the end of fostering, the dogs receive specific service-dog training and get placed with a family.

Could I do that?

There's an e-mail address to write to for more information and even though I'm nearly certain they don't want to hear from twelve-year-olds who don't have $18,000 or permission to be researching a service dog for a family that can't get one because someone's allergic, I write anyway:

Hello.

I saw your dogs at Clay Coves Elementary School. They were amazing. I'm trying to help a family in my neighborhood that really needs a service dog but a person in the family is allergic. Do you train poodles or are there other dogs you train that are okay for people with allergies?

I'm about to press Send when I add:

Also, I was wondering if you could send some information about fostering your puppies because my family might be interested.

I delete the last sentence and write it again and delete it again and then write it again and press Send before I chicken out.

I look outside. It's hard to believe it's going to be stormy anytime soon. The sky's overcast and there's a good breeze, but it's not raining and there's nothing very threatening-looking going on out there. Dad believes the forecast, but Dad also swore this would be the worst winter on record because he saw a woolly bear caterpillar on a tree and its stripes were wide. One of these days I'm going to find his copy of *The Old Farmer's Almanac* and add on to the Twenty Signs of a Hard Winter.

If you see three acorns in a small pile and then hear a bird, look out!

If it's cloudy for four days and then the sun comes out for one hour and you see two butterflies and a squirrel climb a tree, devastation is certain.

Up and down Marigold Street, a lot's going on. The Hunts are pulling a tarp over the table and chairs on their deck and having the hardest time trying to tie a rope around the whole thing. I can't hear them, but Mr. and Mrs. Sanderson are clearly yelling at each other and pointing in different directions in their driveway. Across the street, Irene's husband, Kyle, is wheeling the barbecue grill around the house and into the garage.

A car—Daphne's car—pulls into our driveway.

I run downstairs to meet her.

"JennaLouise wanted to come, but I know you two would turn this into a sleepover and I know your parents are experts at this kind of thing, Army, but I need my girls at home with us when there's a hurricane warning, no offense."

I have no idea how to respond to that.

"Okay, then," Daphne says. "Where should we put all the stuff?"

"There's a spot waiting in the basement," I say. "All the stuff we use to put together the hurricane boxes—it was all in the basement, taking up every bit of space, but we've packed the last boxes. It was serendipity. Did you get a box?"

"Your dad dropped it off yesterday," Daphne says, smiling.

But then her face loses its happiness. "Sweetie, I haven't seen you since Maybe died, and I was so sad to hear about him. You must miss him so much."

"I do." Truest words ever said.

Daphne pulls me close in a quick hug and then walks to the back of the car and opens the hatch. Whoa. It's a party in her trunk! "There's more on the back seat," she says. Two parties! And I see more on the passenger seat in the front!

"But couldn't you use this stuff next time? I mean, I shouldn't take all this if you—"

"I promise, baby, you are doing me a favor. I do not have room, or desire, to store these for another event and that's not how it works, anyway. I was honestly going to lose my mind if it all stayed in my house another minute. It makes me happy that you might be able to use this stuff to help someone."

"But there has to be some way I can repay you. This looks like it cost a fortune, and I might not even need to raise money, because—"

Daphne reaches out for my chin and holds it. She's talking directly into my face. "This was all donated by people and companies that want to do good. I know that you're going to do good. You and I are going to talk about this, about who you're helping and what they need, and we're going to figure it all out."

I nod my agreement as she lets go of my face. JennaLouise's mother gets things done—having her on Team Madison gives me hope.

I grab the hand truck and load three cardboard cartons onto it. Daphne carries a canvas bag filled with children's books and coloring books and we pile everything against the basement wall. And back to the car. Sports equipment! Fancy food! Baking supplies! Crafts! Kids' beach toys. Games and puzzles. It takes four trips to bring in all the giveaways and another two to bring in the baskets and cellophane and ribbons for wrapping. We build piles on the piles of stuff, baskets on top of baskets, against the wall until the empty space is nearly filled up.

"I don't know how to thank you for all this," I say.

"What a coincidence. I don't know how to thank *you* for getting this out of my house. If I had to look at it another minute, there'd have been a gift basket massacre of some kind."

"Which would be too much with a Frankenstorm on the way."

"My daughter has such good taste in friends," Daphne says.

CHAPTER TWENTY-EIGHT

Mom walks in the house right when Dad pulls into the driveway. I say, "Hi, Mom, bye, Mom, heading out with Dad, see you later. Don't be swept away by a storm!"

"Stop jinxing us," Mom mutters as she joins Navy in the kitchen. I hear him ask, "Did you bring me any snacks?" Because that's what storm preparation is all about—providing Navy with Doritos and doughnuts. (As though our parents would ever buy Doritos or doughnuts.)

I go down to the basement and through the door to the garage to meet Dad. When I reach him, he puts his hands on my shoulders and turns my body around, a 180. We walk back into the basement, where he comes to a hard stop. "What have we here?"

"Oh." Hm. I hadn't thought about this part. "Can I explain while we drive? And where are we going?"

"We'll go out to Oldtown and work our way back through Orangeboro. Let me grab something and I'll meet you at the truck."

I run up to my room and check to see if Service with a

Wag has written back. Nothing. I reach in the Maybe box for the picture I stole from Elsie. I'm looking at it, not crying. Which is kind of amazing. I'm still looking when my dad calls, "I'd like to do this today, Army. Before New Jersey washes off the map."

"Stop jinxing us!" Mom yells. I honestly think she believes that saying words can cause our state to fall into the ocean.

I run downstairs. The back of the truck is already packed with hurricane boxes and covered with a tarp, I guess in case it starts raining.

I climb into the cab. "So what's going on in our basement?" Dad asks before I can even turn on the radio.

"JennaLouise's mom was supposed to do some fundraiser that got canceled. And she knew I was, um. Well. Hm."

"You were what?" Dad asks. "What's the first address on there, in Oldtown?"

I grab the clipboard from its spot between the seats. "It's 12 Crosstown Bay."

"And what are those baskets and things for?"

"Well, I'm not exactly sure, but I might do some kind of fundraiser for our neighbors, for Madison's family, the people in the Rooneys' old house." As I say the words, I'm realizing that I forgot to word it so it doesn't sound like, oh, say, sticking my nose where it doesn't belong. Because what I just said sounded very nose-sticky.

"So Dad, what's the latest on the storm?"

"If it hits, it's going to be bad. But we won't likely get the full brunt of it. It was plenty bad in Jamaica and Cuba, though. North Carolina too. But we're not done. You're not done. Tell me about this fundraising idea. Why didn't you and Mom tell me?"

"Um. Mom doesn't know yet, so that's why she didn't. And really, I'm still trying to figure it out. I was talking to Daphne and she had this stuff she couldn't use and I told her I was thinking about trying to do some fundraising events and so she said I'd be doing her a favor if I took it and I guess I thought I'd figure it all out later. And Daphne said she'd help me."

We pull into a driveway. "Want me to run it up?" I ask. Dad nods, so I grab the hand truck and push the box to the front door, grateful for time away from his questions. No one answers when I ring the bell, so I tuck it right against the door, where it'll be protected from rain—if it ever really rains. The strong breeze is turning into serious wind but still, no rain at all.

I climb back in the truck, but Dad doesn't move. "Why did Daphne know about this and your mom and I didn't? What kind of fundraising? Is that family in trouble? And they came to you for help without asking us first? I'm not sure how I feel about that."

"No, Dad. They don't even know. And Daphne didn't know anything until today. There's nothing to know. Except that this family needs help. Madison can break through every lock and she's gotten out of the house without them knowing and they might try alarms on their phones or something and she was on the roof once and—"

Dad puts up his hand, but his face softens. "Army, none of this is making any sense to me. If Irene's family doesn't know, then what makes you think you should be doing this, whatever it is you're doing?"

"All I know is they need help. They need a magic dog, I mean, you know, a service dog, but her husband is allergic and then I remembered about Aunt Emily and Strudel, so I wrote to ask about a poodle and then—"

"Wrote to who? You know what? Let's get going. Let's concentrate on finishing up before this storm hits. We'll have all night to sort this out. Tell me the next address on the list."

The roads are nearly empty as we drive, delivering emergency-supply boxes to clients all over the county. By the time we get back to Clay Coves, it's raining. Hard.

Which is too bad, because Mom hasn't shut the storm shutters yet. I have to help Dad get that done in the rain. It feels like the world is saying, *You didn't think it was going to rain, Army Morand? How's this for rain? And how about this?* We do the first floor and then I hold the ladder so Dad can do the windows on the second floor. By the time we're done, I'm cold and soaked. I take a very long hot shower in the bathroom Navy and I share, which has a shower stall—not a tub filled with hurricane's-coming water.

Navy and Mom have done all the prep they can—battery-operated lanterns and flashlights lined up on the counter, box of candles out on the bench in the mudroom, drinking water in pitchers. Radio with a spare set of batteries on Dad's desk.

Right in the middle of dinner, when the wind and rain don't even seem that bad, the power goes out. "If it's still out in the morning, I'll get the generator going," Dad says, all matter-of-fact. This *is* his business. "There's no telling how long power will be out, and we don't really need it just yet."

He's right. We light the lanterns. And I don't really know why everyone was so worried, because except for the quiet of no TV, the night isn't all that different. Dad keeps the radio on for weather updates, but other than that, it feels kind of like a regular night except we're using flashlights and lanterns. Dad doesn't bring up the fundraising stuff, so neither do I. Sure it's rainy, and a little cold. And windy, and darker, but everything else is just fine.

CHAPTER TWENTY-NINE

I sleep and wake and sleep and wake and my face is so cold. When did it get so cold? I burrow all the way under the blankets. The storm is loud and it sounds kind of scary. There's comfort in the weight of all these blankets—it reminds me of that lead apron the dentist uses when taking X-rays—I always want to ask if I can take it home with me. But there are probably rules against that. Ugh, I hate the dentist. Why am I thinking about the dentist?

Why am I even awake? Oh right, the storm. It's so loud. I wish it would stop already. Will the power be out for days? Will school be closed Monday? Like some kind of snow day even though it's still just October? But if school's closed I'll miss Art and I'm in the middle of sketching a fox and it's the first good thing I've done and if I don't have Art this week, then it'll have to wait another whole week unless I can go to the Art room during lunch and get some work done and why am I thinking about school when I should be sleeping? And really, it would be pretty nice if school is closed on Monday.

And so goes my brain—in and out, around and

back—into dreams and out, with wind-blown rain *swoosh-tat-tat-tat, swoosh-tat-tat-tat*ting against the shutters and roof, startling me awake over and over.

Somehow, through the five-blanket-and-one-pillow barrier, I hear something other than storm noise, a sound that demands attention, demands actual waking. It's knocking. Furious, mean-business knocking. Frantic, desperate. There's a voice with it. I hear the word *help*. Is it *we need help*?

A flashlight's beam cuts through the darkness in the hall and Dad is sort of yell-muttering, "Coming, I'm coming. Hold on," as his feet pad quickly down the stairs. And then the sound of the door and a tumble, almost, inside. I can't place the voice. "We're flooded and our generator stopped working."

I can't make out the rest of the conversation, but really, I cannot believe someone came to our house *in the middle of the night* to tell us about their generator.

I have to see who it is. I wrap a blanket around me, grab my flashlight, and walk downstairs.

It's Linda. And she is dripping all over our entryway. And still talking. "We just didn't think the storm . . . I mean, we've never flooded. Now everything's soaked, so we brought the kittens upstairs and we're trying everything to keep them warm, but our generator wouldn't start and we knew you have one and we were just so desperate . . ."

"Actually, we were planning to get through the night and start it up in the morning, to conserve fuel, so . . ."

Linda's raincoat is plastered to her body, and every part

of her is dripping—her hair, flat against her head, creating little puddles on the mat. The sound of the storm is different down here. In my room, I heard the rain hitting hard against the storm shutters and the roof. Down here, I understand why people talk about wind howling.

"Would you have any idea why our generator isn't working?" Linda asks.

"Every model I've worked with has been different, so I couldn't really guess without spending some time with it," Dad says. "I'd be happy to come over in the morning and give it a look."

"That would be great. Thank you."

Even though it's dark except for those things in the path of the flashlight, I'm struck by the realization that Dad and I are standing in pajamas while our neighbor stands in puddles on the floor. The bed is calling to me—*Come back! I have five blankets! You belong up here with me!*

"Do you want me to walk you home?" Dad asks, maybe because it seems like Linda doesn't realize yet that it's time to go. I want to grab hold of him, to not let him go out into all that heavy rain and wind and, above all, the absolute blackness of the night.

"No sense in that," she says. "Wish me well!" and before we can, she tries to open the door, but the wind seems to want to keep her from doing that. Finally, she sets out into the storm. I hope the kittens are okay.

"Good night again, Dad," I say.

"What next?" he asks.

It sounds like a jinxy thing to say—Mom would think he was inviting trouble just by saying those words—but instead of pointing it out, I go back upstairs to bed, under my blanket mountain.

I am in bed. It is cold and dark and I am aware in some sloggy, sleepy part of my brain that the storm is intense and wild and strong. The wind has moved past whistling and howling to something flat-out furious, like chaos itself is blowing, causing branches and shutters to bang and crash and crack and smash. It's still dark and who even knows what's actually going on out there—it's all clanging and scratching and on top of it rain pelts in angry bursts that sound like waves breaking on the roof. It feels impossible that this storm will remain outside. I imagine shutters blown right off the house, windows shattering into harsh, sharp angles, doors forced down by charging floodwater.

Through all that, there's something else. Within the house Dad's voice carries through the darkness, and he's cursing.

Out of bed, covers off, immediately longing for covers back on; the cold in the house rushes right through my skin straight to my bones. I flick on the light switch to hunt for a sweatshirt but of course, no lights, no power. Only storm.

I find a flashlight, fumble around in the closet until I feel the fuzz of slippers, and slide my feet inside, expecting warmth, grateful for it before I even feel it but no, still freezing. I grab a sweatshirt and head downstairs, gripping the rail carefully. I hear both Mom and Dad now—their voices, not words. Where are they? Not in the kitchen, not in the living room. The door to the basement is a little open, but why would they go down there?

"Hello?" I call, but the storm is slamming its loudness against the house, drowning me out. I take a few steps down and see the hint of light in the corner. Down the last few steps and on the last, what the ... what is . . . *what*? Cold, wet, gross. Freezing, freezing water. Soaking through the bottom of my slippers. Mom and Dad are standing in water, both wearing their rubber boots.

"Dad!?"

"Army, we flooded," he says.

"I thought we never flooded."

"I started to think how Linda said the same thing, that their basement never flooded before but has now, so I got up to check ours."

Exhausted, longing for bed, for bed on a better day in a house with heat, a world not storming, feet not freezing and soaked, I wish I'd never climbed out of bed and that is when I remember.

But—

"Dad? My stuff? The gifts and things Daphne brought over?"

I shine my flashlight beam on his face, knowing that of course he'll have good news, because when you're trying to do a really helpful thing it can't all be wiped out by one stupid rainstorm. But Dad's face tells me everything—it's gray in this bleak basement and his eyes are filled with concern and then he turns.

I follow him and his flashlight and I know it before I see it—and I could kick myself, or something worse than a kick. I could just beat the stuffing right out of myself. The floor? I put Daphne's stuff on the floor instead of the table. Where now the bottoms of everything are soaked through and even more than just the bottoms. The tops of Monopoly Junior and Clue and Sorry are swollen with water, even though they're plastic-wrapped. The baskets that were on the ground are ruined. The bag of books is filled with swollen pages, destroyed, soaked on the bottom, falling apart. It's a snapshot of ruin.

Dad says, "Take my flashlight and grab the laundry baskets and bailing buckets and we'll try to save the things on top before the flood gets worse."

Mom says, "You'll need to put on your rubber boots first."

Can they seriously Never Happened this stuff back into usable gifts? For real?

I turn to head upstairs to get my boots but I slip—it's wet and slippery—and I drop the flashlight. It crashes on my OW! OW!!!! On my toe. OW!! I bend over, trying to hold in the pain, absorb the pain, or basically not die from the pain because it is one heavy flashlight and my poor foot had no idea what was about to happen.

"Are you okay? Army? Are you?" Dad waves a beam of light in my face.

I nod fast but I can't speak. It hurts! *Hurts!* I hunch over until the pain eases to a throbbing ache. I reach down for Dad's flashlight and find it dead. My foot killed the flashlight.

I burst into tears.

"Come on, Army," Mom says, not sounding as impatient with my crying as she usually does. "Let's get to work."

"Why bother?" I pick up the disintegrating cardboard of two giant puzzle boxes. "There's no saving this."

"Not that, no," Mom says, her voice carefully gentle, not maddeningly fake-patient and slow. "But this is what we do. We salvage. We make the best of bad situations."

And even though I know Mom is being extra kind, there's some red anger boiling inside that keeps growing, and I can't keep it from gushing out. "But why can't we do better? It seems like all you do, all we do is patch things up, dry things out, make the worst disappear. Why can't we ever stop the bad from happening in the first place?"

Why am I so mad? Why am I thinking about Elsie Jenkins listing rhyming emotions that day at the beach? "You'll feel sad. You'll feel mad . . ."

"You can't prevent a storm, Army," Dad says. "The best you can do is be prepared."

"Well, I failed at that!" My eyes go from the packs of games and puzzles, all swollen cardboard, to the ruined cellophane and ribbons to the sports equipment, the tape on a tennis racket soaked and hanging off in a creepy little snake coil, and settle on a plastic pail filled with pails, shovels, sand sifters, and castle forms. That one, at least, should be okay.

Mom stands right in front of me and waits until I'm looking directly at her. "Is that what this is all about? You're trying to prevent something bad from happening? To Madison and her family?" I nod. I nod and nod. "Oh, honey. That's way too much for you to take on by yourself, but I understand why you want to try."

The choking sobs stop, but tears are still dripping down, splashing dots on my sweatshirt. All my sadnesses—Maybe, Madison, the ruined gifts from Daphne—are running together, building into something bigger, something that feels like it's rising, and it's just too much. "I didn't keep Maybe safe. It's my fault he died. It should never have happened."

Mom pulls me into a hug.

"Even when we're doing our best, when we make no mistakes, accidents happen," Mom says. "And they're sometimes devastating. I wish that weren't true, but it is. Right now, though, you look exhausted. Dad and I will take the first shift of this. You should go back to bed. We'll get everything that's not ruined on the table and tomorrow we'll get the pump going and deal with the rest of it."

Grateful, but still so sad, I climb back up the basement steps, hearing the storm rage on, miserable and fierce.

CHAPTER THIRTY

The quiet almost seems to have a weight to it. When I wake, there's that moment of knowing something's out of whack but not quite remembering what it is. I kind of don't want to open my eyes, though I'm not sure why. So I stay in bed, cuddled in a C-shape against the wall, under piles of blankets. My foot is throbbing.

So cold.

Why so cold?

No heat.

Why no heat?

Why my morning brain speak like this?

The storm.

It was the storm.

And the flashlight that smashed my toe.

And all that stuff in the basement from Daphne, all that stuff for some kind of fundraiser for Madison's someday magic poodle dog. All that ruined stuff.

I move slowly, swing my feet around so they're hanging off the bed. I reach into the sock drawer for some

Christmas-present fuzzy socks and pull them on. Then my hand finds the mittens Mrs. Rooney made me. I wonder how she's doing in Maine. I think about the afternoons when we shared cookies and tea, when I sat in her house, yarn wrapped around my hands, and listened to stories about her grandkids.

And that, for some reason, makes me reach for Maybe's box, and the baby picture of Maybe. The one I stole from Elsie's house.

When power's back and the world is normal again, I'm going to force myself to give it back. It almost feels as though the world's been off, tilted a little wrong or something, since I took it.

But I have it now, so I lift the window shade for some light. Oh right. Storm shutters. Ugh, look at that—one of the storm shutters over my window is hanging on by just one corner. But it provides light so I can look into the dark eyes of the puppy that would grow to be my sweet Maybe. As I stare at the round puppy shape, it's impossible not to think about the puppies I saw on that website. Fostering a puppy. Probably not possible but not definitely impossible. Baby steps. Progress. Moving, slowly, in the right direction.

I try the switch on the wall, which is stupid, as the house is absolutely freezing and surely if we had power, it wouldn't be.

I tuck the photo in the box and start to get dressed because I want to go outside. No, it's more like need. I need to go out. I pull on layers of clothes, hoping to warm up. I have to see what this storm did to my world.

My parents are talking in the kitchen, so I head that way. But it's actually just Mom, talking to herself as she writes a list. The sun is streaming in the kitchen window over the sink. In a post-storm world, things could be worse.

I stare at Mom, just waiting, because she does not like to have her concentration broken. She has her glasses on and gives a tiny nod in my direction. After another minute she puts the pencil down.

"Dad opened the storm shutters on the first floor and he's trying to get the generator going to pump out the basement." She smiles and takes a deep breath, a sigh. "You sleep okay?"

I nod, even though I was wakened by a neighbor and then again when my plans for helping Madison got flooded and ruined.

"I'm hungry!" I didn't even know it, but man alive, it's true! I go to the refrigerator and Mom screams, "You can't open it! We have too much stuff in there—I don't want to lose it. We need to keep the cold in."

I've heard this before, but this is the first time I've realized how dumb it is. "If it might go bad anyway, wouldn't it make sense to eat some first, so we can at least use some food for, like, what it was intended for?" The truth is there's nothing so delicious in there that I'd be sad to lose it.

Mom shakes her head. "I'd rather you take something from the pantry, a breakfast bar or cereal or something?"

I pour some water from the pitcher on the table into a glass and walk to the living room window.

Overnight, the world has changed. Yesterday—hours ago—some trees still had the last of their strong steeped reds, yellows, oranges. Now they are winter-bare. Up and down the block, so many trees—eight, nine, ten—look like they were mutilated, limbs snapped from their trunks. A giant aqua pool noodle tangled with a jagged branch. A child's ride-on fire engine, its light broken in red plastic pieces on the waterlogged grass.

I'm not sure what I was expecting—rowboats out front, helicopters hovering, looking for people to rescue, news crews, police. But it seems quiet.

I really need to get out. Like, I am *buzzing* with a need to be outside.

Mom says, "Wait for your brother." How does she know what I'm thinking? From all the way in the kitchen?

"Navy can find me," I say, turning the doorknob.

"Army, wait."

I pace. I feel this nearly electric need to not be in the house, to be out. And then I think of Madison. I wonder if this is how she felt when she climbed out the window—a humming, whirring pulse practically trying to push me right out the door. Is this anything like how she feels when she's kept from doing what she needs to be doing?

Navy finally comes rushing down the stairs in what he is too old to call his yellow stompy boots, grabs a cereal bar, and then finally, we're outside!

Instead of the quiet I expected, there's that loud,

in-your-face loud, mechanical hum. Dad has the generator going. I walk around to the driveway and sure enough, there he is.

Navy waves to Dad as he and I head in an odd stepping-over-small-branches dance out to the street.

"Whoa, whoa, whoa," Dad yells. "Did Mom go over everything? The live-wire situation in particular?"

"We know, Dad," Navy says. "Live wires can kill you. Keep your eyes peeled—that's really gross—and let an adult know if you spot one."

Dad looks proud. There's nothing like a serious disaster to make him feel good.

As we start walking up the block, we cringe at the sight of trees fallen sideways, resting on the roofs of the Hunts' house and Mr. Sherman's. A tangled pile of trampoline nets lies in a heap in the Hunts' front yard. The trampoline's not there—just the net.

I have this urge to go check on Madison, to make sure all is well. But she has both parents with her. And what I really need is to be walking around outside, not stuck in a house. Maybe I'll stop by later.

An old rocking chair—it could be from Mr. Hoffart's porch—far from its home, crashed against the green metal post of a stop sign. The satellite TV dish that used to be on the Sandersons' roof is lying mostly on the hood of Mr. Sanderson's yellow Jeep. I stumble and then—ew! My rain boot is covered by a black plastic cover—from a barbecue grill? It's grossly slimy, and I make a mental note to wash my hands as soon as I get home so I don't get some hurricane disease.

We're walking slowly. The air is weird—chilly and gray, but there's a hint of that strong almost-summer-like humidity, a heaviness that feels out of place in fall.

"I'll bet this is how scary movies start out," Navy says. "Two kids. A big storm. Horrible scariness."

It *is* spooky that we're the only ones out.

"I hope everything's back to normal by tomorrow," Navy says.

I laugh. The neighborhood is absolutely wrecked. "What's tomorrow? Also, no. It won't be."

"Tomorrow my class is making Halloween snacks with our kindergarten buddies. Are you saying there won't be school tomorrow?"

I shrug because I can't be certain. But it's pretty clear that this world, as it is now, is not the kind in which little kids should be outside, walking to school. It's hard to believe things will even be back to normal by Wednesday, in time for Halloween.

When we turn the corner, I see giant Henrietta, one of my favorite neighborhood dogs, slowly trotting from tree to tree, happy to be outside. She spots me and tears loose of her owner to come say hello. I run toward her too, give her a huge hug, my arms wrapped around her sweet brown neck. I pull her head close, scratch behind her ears, under her chin. And then Henrietta gets me with that fat dog tongue. Oh, dog kisses. Oh, dogs. Henrietta leaves me for a second to explore Navy, but then comes right back and leans her ear, hard, into my hand, just in case I forgot where she likes to be scratched. Her owner—the man (Henrietta is walked equally by a man and a woman) asks how we're doing, when we lost power, if we have any idea when it's coming back. Because kids are usually the first to know? I hold on to Henrietta as long as I can and then wrap my arms tighter around her one more time to say goodbye, breathing in her dog-fur smell. Oh, Henrietta!

"Which way should we go?" Navy asks as Henrietta walks away.

"I'm not sure."

So we just keep going straight. Until we get to Mr. Hoffart's house, where I see the funniest thing. Or not funny, but unexpected.

Elsie Jenkins. There's Elsie Jenkins, walking toward Mr. Hoffart's house.

"Hey," I say, "Elsie Jenkins! I mean, Elsie!"

"Oh, hey, Army." She turns around. And—does she seem embarrassed?

"This is my brother, Navy," I say. "Navy, this is Elsie Jenkins. Elsie. You met her at Cub Scouts once."

"Jenkins like the vet?" Navy asks.

The kid can't memorize a basic fact for a history test. His grades make our father's face turn the kinds of colors that cartoon characters turn before they explode. But this, the vet's name, the vet he met only once or twice, this he can recall instantly. The name that makes me squirm and tear up. Wow.

Elsie smiles and says, "Yeah. She's my mom."

In an effort to change the topic immediately (thank you so much, Navy), I ask, "How do you know Mr. Hoffart? Were you going to check on him?"

Elsie does a really impressive impersonation of my father's face-color changing.

"Yes."

But she doesn't move.

"Do you want me to go with you?" I ask.

"I just have to tell you—I used to see you bring his newspaper to him when you'd walk your dog—you can see his house from my bedroom window." She points up the hill, as though she needs to prove it. "And then I noticed that you weren't doing it, so I thought I'd do it until you get back to it. And today I just wanted to make sure he was okay."

Elsie!! Taking care of Mr. Hoffart! "Does he know it's you?"

She shakes her head fast. "No. I don't know why, but I thought it would be better if he thought you were still doing it."

"He never knew it was me," I say. We both almost laugh, a sound closer to a double hiccup.

And then Navy says, "What are you guys talking about?"

"The guy who delivers newspapers just throws Mr. Hoffart's here, at the top of his driveway," Elsie says. "But Mr. Hoffart's such an old guy—"

"And it takes him like twenty minutes from when he leaves his house until he gets the paper and goes back in, so—"

"So we just do it for him." And then she smiles at me.

And I feel it very clearly that yes, this *is* a friendship, a real one.

"I am so sorry, Elsie, but I took something from your house. It was a picture of—"

"Your dog. When he was a puppy. I know. I was going to give it to you, or ask you if you wanted it, but it's so hard to bring things up and—"

I grab Elsie's wrist and squeeze it. "You knew I took it? And you were going to give it to me? You must think I'm the most—"

"All I think is that you needed that picture. And I'm glad you have it."

We link arms and start walking toward Mr. Hoffart's front door together, Navy a few steps behind. We stop to pick up twigs and a bigger branch and two empty water bottles that have found their way to his blacktop driveway, reminding me of that day at the beach cleanup. And making me long for a pair of gloves. Ew.

I don't know Mr. Hoffart well, but I do know this is the kind of thing one ought to do after a big storm, check on older neighbors to make sure they're okay. I guess I always pictured an adult doing it, but if Mr. Hoffart needs help of any kind, I can get someone.

So I ring the bell and we wait. When he opens the door, he doesn't seem surprised exactly. Is he amused?

"And what have we here?" he says, with the start of a smile. That's what my dad always says!

"Hi, Mr. Hoffart. My friend Elsie and I, and my brother, Navy—we just wanted to make sure you're okay, see if you need anything."

"I've been listening to my portable radio. Roads are impassable." Is that a word? Or does he not know how to say *impossible*?

"But you're okay?" Elsie asks.

"Yes, of course. My daughter will be by to check on me, I'm sure, as soon as the roads are again passable."

Oh. *Passable. Impassable.* Right.

"Okay," I say. "If you need anything, though, you could let us know."

"Well, I can't call you, because my phone doesn't work. So how about if I whistle really loud?"

I think he's playing around with us. And that our work here is done. I say, "Sounds like a plan!"

And then Elsie puts her fingers in her mouth and lets out this loud, traffic-stopping (if roads were passable) whistle. Mr. Hoffart takes two steps back and laughs. "That's one fine whistle," he says. "And by the way, thanks for bringing my newspaper. Both of you."

Elsie and Mr. Hoffart are both full of surprises.

CHAPTER THIRTY-ONE

So now our sort of aimless, no-plan walk through the nature's war-zone version of our neighborhood includes Elsie too. She doesn't ask, just follows when Navy and I continue on. I think of Dorothy gathering friends along her way down the yellow brick road.

Navy spots his friend Cullen in his front yard with his dad. "Hi, Mr. Forester," I say.

"Hey there, Army. Navy."

Navy joins Cullen on the lawn. Almost instantaneously, they start to build something with the sticks, branches, and twigs gathered there.

"Your folks survive the storm okay?" Mr. Forester asks.

"Our basement flooded, but we're fine," I say.

"Do you think your parents would be okay with Navy staying with us for a while?" he asks.

"Yes!" Navy shouts before Cullen's dad even finishes asking.

"I'm sure it'll be fine," I say. "I'll let them know."

Elsie and I continue on, having left the Scarecrow or Tin

Man or whatever at his friend's house. Up ahead, Johnny on the Spot is looking kind of frantic, running over to talk to Henrietta's man, loud and fast. I hear him say, "The girl, Madison. She's missing."

I glance at Elsie and she's . . . I thinks the word's *aghast,* but she looks somewhere between *aghast* and *aghost,* because she's gone pale and her mouth is wide open. Johnny says, "We're getting everyone out to find her." He takes off.

"We'll cover more ground if we split up," I say to Elsie.

"I don't even know what Madison looks like."

"She's little, like six or seven maybe, blond hair, and, oh my God, this is just . . ." I start walking away.

"Wait!" she says.

I turn back to face her. But I need to go. I need to look for Madison. "I'm sorry. Can you just help look for her?" She's nodding as I turn and walk down the middle of the street. There are no cars, just the damage caused by wind and rain and the force of an angry storm. But no cars. That's a good thing. Madison can't be hurt in that one way. Just in all the others.

Above the voice of generators, I hear a voice calling: "Madison! Madison? Madison!!!"

If that person knew her at all, he'd know she won't respond to someone calling her name. It's probably making it even less likely we'll find her.

My feet keep moving me forward as I peek around corners and look up to the tops of things, hoping to see, needing to see Madison, needing her to be okay.

I'm breathing too fast. I remind myself what Irene said about Madison's good sense of direction, how she used the *ch ch ch* sound to direct her mother to the park that day. Madison is smart! She can find her way home.

My mother is running toward me.

"Did they find her?" I ask.

Mom's face is tight and worried. "Where's Navy?"

"He's at Cullen's. Is Dad out too?" I ask.

"Actually, he's in their house with the babies."

Should I go take his place? No, I need to find Madison.

"Be careful, Army," Mom says.

"Look *up* for her. She likes to be up."

I climb over the massive trunk of a felled tree, then over a broken-looking motorcycle on its side. I scan trees, neighbors' yards, behind hedges.

Two blocks away, I see what I think is the Hunts' trampoline. How could it have flown or rolled or bounced so far?

Anything is possible.

Madison, where did you go?

When I pass my mom and Henrietta-the-dog's man-walker again, they shake their heads at me: *No. No, we don't have her. No, she's still gone.* I think I spot Madison's father down the street, but by the time I catch up, he's not there.

I have no idea what Madison knows and what she doesn't, but I bet there's a really good chance Madison doesn't know a thing about live wires. She can't be alone out in this whole big world. She just can't. Is she feeling, *Oh no, I'm lost,* or is she thinking, *Finally!* Or is she not thinking the way I think at all? Maybe she's just content to be where she is—more like, *Ahhh. This. Now.*

A new sound rises above the generators—a siren. Loud and urgent. And then of course I realize: *Oh my God, an ambulance. Oh my God, Madison.*

My brain is a slide show of terror.

Madison near a live wire.

Madison up a tree.

Madison in the street.

Madison out alone in this slick and unstable world.

Madison being wheeled into an ambulance.

Which street is the noise coming from?

And there it is, the ambulance, moving slowly. Slower than I've ever seen an ambulance move. I once read that ambulances only move slowly when the person inside has died.

But no. It's stopped now. It can't get through.

Neighbors are spread out in front of it—clearing a path, getting debris and tree parts out of the way so the ambulance can reach its destination, whatever that is. I'm grateful they're doing this and that there's now something I can do with my hands, a way to help.

I run up next to Mr. Hunt and bend to help lift a branch. It takes both of us and it's hard to grip, because the rough bark is slick with wet and sodden heaviness, but we do and when we set it against the curb, I ask, "Is the ambulance for Madison?"

"I think so," Mr. Hunt says. "I assume so. I heard she was found two streets away. Her mom found her."

The way he says it, it sounds like she might be . . . not okay at all. *Her mom found her.*

The part of my brain that does things automatically may have shut off.

I have to remember to breathe in.

Breathe out.

Breathe in.

Breathe out.

We continue ahead and meet up with a big group of people trying to move another tree that lies across the road. I step in next to Cullen's mom and everyone pushes and lifts and then we move it enough for the ambulance to get by. But all this time, there's something building, a high-pitched terror about why we're doing this, why an ambulance, and then I see my mom.

She rushes toward me. I think of that tiny sliver of time after I came home from school that day, when I looked at her and didn't know what she was going to say, if Maybe was okay. And then she said the worst thing she could say.

But her body language is different this time. She's racing toward me and she says, "Madison's okay. She broke through her window and Irene didn't know because the alarm on her phone didn't go off on her cell. It must have been the cell phone reception. But she's fine. Irene may have broken her leg, something about a slip and fall on a sewer drain when she was walking Madison back home."

Mom comes closer and holds me tight, and I start to breathe properly again. She tells me how after she fell Irene kept trying to call 911 and then finally the call went through.

I tell Mom I have one thing to do before I come home. I start walking again—it's like I've been programmed to walk these streets and now I can't stop. I walk around the neighborhood looking for Elsie but not finding her. I go to her house and she hugs me when I tell her that Madison is okay.

CHAPTER THIRTY-TWO

My father is the master of generators. He switches power from one appliance to another. He posts a schedule about when the generator will be on, so neighbors can charge their cell phones, laptops, whatever they need, on the power strips and extension cords in our driveway. But he also turns it off, to conserve the fuel. Most cell phones are working now, even though some cell towers were knocked out.

When the generator is on, our house starts to resemble what I imagine the Clay Coves Inn to be like—the real one, not Mr. Sherman's house.

Dad also fixed Linda and Sue's generator but they quickly ran out of diesel fuel and now two days after the storm, we're almost out too.

We've heard that roads are slowly being cleared, but we have no idea when we can get more diesel fuel.

Lots of cleanup calls have been coming in, but until roads are cleared, my parents are stuck at home.

I've been trying not to check my phone every ten minutes,

but I can't help it. I haven't heard back from Service with a Wag. They're probably busy after the storm too.

Almost everyone is home. School is canceled in our town and all the ones nearby until power is restored. My parents are hoping they'll be called in to help restore Oceanside Elementary one town over, where, rumor has it, hundreds of pounds of dead fish flooded the school and five live sea turtles were found swimming in the hallways. What do those five turtles make of the flags in the corners of each room? The jack-o'-lanterns taped to the insides of classroom windows?

Irene came home from the hospital yesterday and she texted to ask if I could come by to help out. When I told Mom, she smiled and said, "Ask them if they need anything else. If there's anything more we can do to help."

I went over again today. It's so cold, but luckily I have those red mittens Mrs. Rooney made me. I rarely take them off.

Madison's dad is home, and at least when I've been there, he's been filling his time by yelling questions at Irene. "Where's that cream that you use for a rash?" "How long should I let Schuyler sleep?" "What do you do when that dirty diaper thing is full and does it always reek like that?" Each time, Irene asks him to stop yelling, to come into the bedroom and speak to her there, where she's resting in bed.

I've been spending a lot of time with the babies. I move them between the swing and play mat, to their cribs for naps.

I read them board books. I've even learned how to change diapers. It's exactly as gross as I thought it would be.

Madison's parents got her an iPad before the storm and she's always busy on it, doing something (I'm not sure what). My favorite thing that happened was when Madison showed me a picture, a little-kid-book illustration of a dog. I thought back to sitting on the roof with her. Did she show me that because of what I told her about Maybe? Or just because it's a cute picture. Either way, it made me smile.

"Army, hon, would you come in here for a minute?" Irene calls from her bedroom after I've put the twins in their cribs.

Irene's sitting up in bed, her leg propped up on two pale green pillows, with a tray—like a breakfast-in-bed tray—over her lap. She has piles of papers neatly stacked in front of her. "I've finally gotten to this paperwork. Once school reopens, I'm going to enroll Madison."

"Do you think she'll like school?"

Irene smiles. "I have no idea. That girl is full of surprises."

"I've liked getting to spend some time with her," I say.

"You've been so good to us, Army, and I hate to ask more of you, but I do have one favor. I've been trying to figure something out—Kyle wants to take the babies trick-or-treating with those neighbors, Stevie and that little girl . . ."

"Bella," I say. "So you heard about the rescheduled Halloween? That everyone's trick-or-treating Friday?"

"Yes. And so if he goes out, then Madison and I are here and people will be coming to the door and I'm not moving around so well yet. And with Madison, I'm just worried about all the noise and excitement."

"I can come over and help, sure." JennaLouise and I both think that no one should trick-or-treat after sixth grade. I plan to just steal some candy from Navy. "Does Madison do anything special for Halloween?"

Irene shakes her head. "Oh no. But having you here. That will be a treat in itself. Thanks so much."

"Can I ask *you* a question?"

Irene smiles, reaches behind her back to straighten the pillow. "Anything."

"I know you said your husband is allergic to dogs. Did you ever try a dog with hair, not fur? Like a poodle? My aunt Emily has a poodle and she's allergic to most dogs but not to this one. She's had Strudel for eight years."

Irene just looks at me. "What is that mind of yours thinking, Army? Do you have a dog?"

"I did," I say. "He died, right around when you moved here. His name was Maybe and he was the best." I think I'm done, but then I say, "I miss him."

"Do you have pictures? I'd love to see him," Irene says.

I nod but I need to say what I have to say. "But the thing about poodles is . . . they can be trained as service dogs. Like for Madison."

I tell Irene what service dogs can do. About little Sawyer, whose dog, Scout, found him when he walked away from his grandmother's house. How Sawyer has a loyal and loving service dog right by his side every day to help keep him safe.

"There's a place near us," I say, "called Service with a Wag. The dogs cost a lot of money, that's the hard part, and also there's a really long wait to get one, but my best friend JennaLouise's mother is an event planner and Clay Coves Community Day is coming up and she's going to help me organize a fundraiser there—other ones too—if you think it's a good idea." I take a breath and stop talking because of the look Irene's giving me. "What?"

"I knew it when we met," Irene says. "You *are* an army of one. I'm always interested in anything that can make life easier for Madison. So let me learn more about these dogs. About all of it." She pauses for a second and then asks, "Is there anything you can't do?"

"Plenty," I say. "Most things." But inside I feel a little hum of happiness that's growing a bit louder and stronger.

As I'm leaving, I realize something. That part of me has been thinking that helping Madison's family has something to do with what I *didn't* do for Maybe—that I couldn't keep my dog safe, so I need to keep this girl safe. But of course, no. Not at all. That connection only exists in my brokenhearted brain.

There's no erasing what happened. There's no way to balance it out.

But finding a magic dog for Madison still feels like what I need to do. That it's up to me to help someone I care about, even if it's someone I don't know all that well.

CHAPTER THIRTY-THREE

The next day the power still hasn't come on but luckily my parents heard about a gas station that has power and received a delivery. They decided to see if the roads were clear and they were. After two hours of waiting, they got more diesel for the generator—there are limits to how much you can get, so they both went, in the truck and the car. There's no way to know how long this will last.

Mom and Dad spend the morning driving to the clients' homes they can get to, but without electricity in those homes, there's only so much they can do now. They order dumpsters to be delivered once things are back to normal, help with what they can, but the bulk of the work will have to wait until the electricity is back on. Mom is getting a little stir-crazy.

"Let's go," Mom says to me, grabbing the keys to the car.

"Where to?" I ask. Likely answers include Home Depot, Food City, the dump to get rid of stuff.

"Passenger's pick," she says.

We wave to Dad and Navy in the driveway as we walk

out to the car, parked in front of the house. "Where's Passenger's Pick?"

Mom shakes her head like I'm a little bit of an idiot. "You are the passenger. You pick."

Right.

I have an idea. "I'm going to put an address in, and it's somewhere I really want to go if the roads are clear, but could we keep it a surprise until we get there? I think it's like twenty minutes away."

"I'm game. Let's go. Anywhere but here."

I have all the info in my phone, so I enter the address and we head out toward the great unknown: Service with a Wag.

If I ask myself, "Am I ready for this?" the answer is no. So I don't ask. I just go. Keep moving in the right direction. Or in some direction. It has to be better than standing still.

For some reason Mom seems content to look out the window, to follow the directions Deirdre (that's what I named my GPS app's voice) gives. Until she says, "You know this time off from school might be a good opportunity for you to get your room organized."

I look at her like she must be kidding.

She is not kidding.

"I like it the way it is. We . . . we're different like that."

"You mean the way you're more naturally a slob and I'm—" Her face is kind, even if her words aren't that nice. But it's true. I tend toward slob. Just in my room though.

"But Mom, it's not just that. Things—things that don't mean a lot to you—can mean something to me."

"So that box of papers from second grade in your closet means something?"

"Yeah," I say. "But I mean other things. Like Maybe's things. You got rid of all his stuff before I could even take what I wanted to remember him."

She looks ahead. I can almost hear her trying to stay quiet until she says with a little laugh, "That would have been everything."

"So?" I ask. "What's wrong with that? I loved him. I miss him. I wanted some of his things."

"But they're just things. You have your memories, and I knew it would be easier for you to get over it without all the reminders around."

"For you," I say. "That's what's easier for you. For me, it helps to have an actual thing that's part of the memory. The *things* have meaning to me." And not just to me. I think of Elsie Jenkins and her father's ring around her neck.

She's quiet. She nods. "When my father died, I helped my mother pack up his things, all of them. It's what she said you do, and so we did."

My grandfather died when my mother was thirteen. I never thought of her, of that, the way I think about Elsie and her father. It hurts my heart to imagine little Mom packing her father's clothes and books and watch. Did he have a high school ring?

Deirdre interrupts with directions.

Mom says, "She said to turn here, but this looks like someone's home. Is it someone you know, Army?"

"Not exactly," I say.

Mom turns into a driveway and follows it along until it ends in front of a garage. "Do you not exactly want to explain where we are?"

I really should have thought this through. "So one day I went to pick up Navy from school and he didn't tell me he had Cub Scouts, so I had to sit through the whole meeting and this group, Service with a Wag, was there. They train service dogs. And that fundraiser I need to do for Madison's family is to help them afford one of the dogs. That is if they have poodles or other dogs that are okay for people with allergies."

Mom's face, so confused, would be funny, but she says, "I think it's a good sign that you're thinking about dogs."

I'm shaking my head, ready to explain, when she says, "You know you have to forgive yourself, honey."

A lot of times when my mother tells me what I should do, I have a strong desire to do the opposite. But this time when I hear her words it's not like that at all. It's more—*Wait. I can do that? I can forgive myself?* It stings a little, because I don't think I've earned forgiveness, but I also know I can't keep living with all the guilt. It helps to think it's possible, that I *can* forgive myself.

"I don't know how," I say. "Because I can't do the Never Happened thing—act like there never was a Maybe. That doesn't work, it's not right. I'm glad he existed and I don't want to make him, his memory, disappear."

Mom takes some time with this. Then she says, "I work with people going through awful things. Some are caused by nature, but some are caused by mistake, by human error. People make mistakes. It's part of what being human is. We can learn from them. But it does us no good to not allow ourselves to move on from them, Army."

I'm still trying to think that through, how it would work, moving on while still remembering, when Mom indicates a tall woman with short hair walking to our car with her head tilted to the side.

Mom opens her door. "We're by appointment only," the woman says.

"Sorry," Mom says, stepping out of the truck. But she slides right into Never Happened mode, without so much as an awkward beat. "How'd you fare in the storm?"

"Bad. Very bad," the lady says. "But do I know you? Forgive me, *should* I know you?"

I smile at her as I climb out on my side. "Your dogs visited my brother's Cub Scout troop and I saw them there and they were amazing. And also I wrote to you before the storm, asking if you have service dogs for people with allergies, and—"

"Right. And asking about your family fostering a puppy."

Mom looks at me like... Okay, I have nothing to compare her look to.

There's a kind of silence that might be funny in a movie or on TV, but all I need is for it to end, so I'm very relieved when the woman says, "I'm Marion Chaplain. Can I invite you inside?"

Mom shrugs and I say thank you and we follow Marion into one of the buildings—there are a few, spaced far apart—that look like barns or garages or storage.

I hear the sound of whining puppies before we're even in the building. The building's warm—there's a generator going somewhere—and ripe with animal smell. When we turn the corner, oh my God, a whole playpen filled with puppies.

"May I?" I ask the woman. She nods. And I race over and, okay, I climb right into the playpen with the puppies. I can't keep myself from doing it. And they swarm me. I am puppy-swarmed! The softness! I had forgotten how impossibly soft puppy fur is when they're so young. I sit down in the playpen and they're climbing on me and nibbling and dog-kissing my neck, my hands, my face. I find myself taking in a sharp breath and fear the humiliation—I'm about to cry—but I surprise myself (and the puppies) because a laugh surges right out of my mouth. I'm so loud that one puppy pees on my leg. And it doesn't even bother me!

It's like some medicine I didn't know I needed. When I pause to look up for a second, my mother doesn't look as mortified as I would have guessed. She is shaking her head, but with a big smile. Marion too.

"There's nothing like puppies," Marion says. Marion is so smart.

"These puppies answer the question you asked in your e-mail. I'm sorry—I can't remember your name."

"Oh, no, I'm sorry," I say. "Army. Army Morand."

"Right. You'd think I could remember that name." And then she says to my mother, "No offense," which makes me laugh again. Who knew that all I needed to do to change my crying and worrying into laughter was to climb into a play-pen of puppies!

On my lap, one puppy has settled. He is tan with brown ears. Or she. I have no idea. The rest of the litter keep climbing on me.

"This litter is bred to be hypoallergenic, like you were asking about. I could introduce you to the parents—a poodle and a goldendoodle."

Mom shoots me a look like, *Do you understand everything going on here, because I don't?* I smile. I am, after all, surrounded by puppies.

"And you mentioned fostering and I have a proposition for you." And then Marion turns to my mom. "Well, I imagine really for you, since our contracts need signing by adults. The one in your daughter's lap won't be trained as a service dog. On early screening we learned he has elbow dysplasia, which would keep him from service work. He'll live a normal life, but he can't handle the strain of a harness. We'll be looking for a forever home for him."

I look down in my lap. I'm thinking the words *It looks like you found it* at the exact same time as my mother says them out loud.

"Wait, what?" I say. I haven't decided if I can do this yet, but oh my God, this little fluffball is just perfect and I can't believe my mom said I could keep him. Is that what she said? "Really?"

"Definitely," she says. Which would be a funny name for the dog who follows Maybe. But it's probably time for a member of the Morand family to have a regular, less accidental name.

CHAPTER THIRTY-FOUR

"We usually charge for our non-service dogs, when families adopt them as puppies," Marion says, and I feel the joy start to seep out of me, like a balloon three days after a party. I have money in my bank account, but I had hoped to use some of that to help Madison.

Before Mom or I can respond, Marion continues. "But I wonder if you're open to creative solutions."

That makes me want to laugh, which wouldn't surprise anyone, as I've been laughing and awwwwing, and belly rubbing—the softest puppy bellies in the world. But mostly I've been holding the puppy, the one who hasn't left my lap, with my left hand, stroking his head, gently rubbing his ears, trying to let him know I am someone he can trust. Because I need to believe that, that I can keep this dog safe, and give him so much love. I am trying my hardest to convey all of that with my silent left hand.

"I don't know what your daughter's told you about our service dogs," Marion says. And then the door opens and a man comes in—I recognize him from the Cub Scout meeting. "This is my husband, Bill," Marion says. I smile up at him, unwilling to move because this puppy is never leaving my lap.

"To what do we owe this pleasure?" Bill asks. Which is a lot nicer than *What are these uninvited guests doing here.*

"Well, maybe Band-Aid has found a home."

"Band-Aid?" I say.

"The one in your lap," Bill says.

"We use names to keep them straight while they're here," Marion says. "You're free to change it—they're so young they haven't learned their names yet. I was just about to mention the idea you and I had, Bill, about keeping Band-Aid and Rigby together.

"We don't normally do this, but we find ourselves having to place our pups as soon as possible, as two of our four kennels were flooded in the storm. And our house, the building behind this, had some bad wind damage and flooding too. I was planning to write back to you, Army, and see if we could talk about the possibility of you taking two dogs, if you had any interest in keeping Band-Aid for yourself and fostering Rigby. If the person isn't allergic to Rigby he could be for the family you were talking about. It's very positive if the family receiving the dog is included in some way in the early months of the puppy's training. We'd give you Band-Aid, but you'd have to pay for Rigby if the family ends up taking him."

"I'm not clear what's involved with fostering," Mom says.

"We'll send you home with the information—there's a

lot, and you'll receive all the training information you need. The way it works is you'll need to start the dog on basic training—housebreaking, learning to walk on a leash, basic commands—and getting him used to different kinds of environments. You'll be expected to provide the dog with food, veterinary care, to attend required basic training classes. It's a significant commitment. Our fosters come back here every two months for checkups. And at the end of fostering you'll bring the dog back to Service with a Wag for his special training before he can go to a forever home. You'll need to be sure before you commit. But if it all works out, we would be able to match that family with a dog! You'd bypass our waiting list and have that opportunity earlier than you would if you just signed up now. We're racing to find these dogs homes because the cleanup here is going to take a while and we just don't have the facilities."

"Which one's Rigby?" I ask.

Bill leans down. "The one that's climbing on your back. Here," he says, reaching for the dog and lifting him so I can see. "Have a look."

Oh, Rigby. What a good boy. He's all brown, except the tip of his tail is black. He's reaching for my face, trying to kiss it. Bill puts him down in the pen and the puppy starts climbing up my back again.

And here's where the old worrying me returns. "Mom, even if it turns out that Madison's dad isn't allergic, getting the dog for Madison isn't really a done deal—there's like a ton of money involved. That's why I was planning to do fundraising. Rigby will cost eighteen thousand dollars."

I expect the room to go quiet, and it does. And it's awkward. I have an idea, but I know it's not a good one. But since it is the only one, I say, "Is there any way I could pay you a little at a time? Maybe I could help you? Service with a Wag? Like work for you as a way to pay some of the money for the dog?"

"I'm guessing you don't have your driver's license," Bill says.

It's true. Not a perfect idea.

I happen to be looking at my mom's face, so I see it brighten, right there in front of us all, as an idea occurs to her.

"So let me ask *you*," Mom says. "Are *you* open to creative solutions?"

My brain tries not explode as Mom talks about the services Never Happened provides. *Just feel your warm hand on Band-Aid's head, Army*. And I do. I tell Band-Aid with my left hand that I will be his best friend and do everything I can to keep him safe.

Mom keeps talking. I can't help but wonder what she's thinking, trying to make a sale in the middle of this . . . whatever this is.

"Money's so tight for us right now," Bill says, looking embarrassed. "We're going to try to make do with two kennels until . . . well, for now. Make do for now."

"And that's why I asked if you were open to creative solutions, something of a barter situation."

I know my parents are always saving for things, and they didn't get anywhere near their goal of buying a whole-house generator this year, which we really could use right now. She can't be offering what I think she's offering.

"In other words," Mom continues, "if the service dog works out for Madison's family, Army works for me, because our business is conveniently located in the house where she lives. And my company does the work for you." Bill looks confused. I'm having some trouble figuring it all out too.

My mother continues, "And if you take the cost of our work for you off the price of the service dog, of . . . what did you say that puppy's name was?"

"Rigby," I say. "His name is Rigby."

"And Army will make up any difference with the fundraising she's planning to do. Either way, we'd be happy to take Band-Aid permanently and foster Rigby once we get our power back. That should be some time next week."

I can't believe my mom just agreed to two dogs.

CHAPTER THIRTY-FIVE

When we get back home, Linda is in the driveway, talking with Dad, heavy-looking pillowcases over her shoulders. She and Sue have been stopping by every hour with pillowcases full of dry beans that they heat up in our microwave and then take home to keep the kittens warm. They lay each kitten in a sleeping-bag sock in a cardboard box filled with warm beans. Dad has the microwave set up right in the garage so they have easy access. They've also gone house to house, gathering up shoeboxes. Navy asked if they're making dioramas. I hope he's kidding—does Navy really think adults have to make dioramas?

Even though I'm buzzing with puppy promise, I'm feeling done with this post-Frankenstorm world. Most people are still home because the places where they work have no power. Johnny on the . . . no—Mr. Elkton's white truck drives by again. I've already seen him hauling half a sailboat, three wooden doors, part of a dock, and what looks like a big piece of an aboveground pool. And now an enormous lifeguard chair, more than half hanging off the back of the truck, secured with crisscrossed ropes.

More exciting than that, Margaret Ann is pulling into the driveway to drop off JennaLouise. Finally! It feels like forever since I've seen her. And though she wasn't invited—this is not surprising—Elsie's marching toward my house too.

Elsie's still out of earshot when JennaLouise, out of the car, asks, "What's Elsie Jenkins doing here?"

"She shows up a lot," I say.

"Oh," JennaLouise says, "if this is going to be one of those Elsie-Jenkins-and-Army-together times, I can just call Margaret Ann to come back and get me and—"

"No," I say. "Stop. We're good. You and me. This is just . . ." How on earth does a person explain Elsie Jenkins? I mean Elsie. "Maybe give her a chance?" I say.

"Really?" she asks. And I get it. Elsie Jenkins, for a really long time, was an oddity like Marcus the sniffer. And I should probably stop calling him that too. Marcus. Elsie.

I nod yes, and beam her a *please?* from my eyes.

She gives me a small nod as she hands me a piece of paper. "My mom said to fill out this form to get a table at Clay Coves Community Day. And she said you can just bring it to Mr. Sherman's house and he'll get it to the right people before the deadline. It's supposed to cost something like a hundred dollars, but Mom knows people and she said they'll let you have it for free."

"Thanks," I say. "And I have this petition I need you to sign when we go inside."

I'm looking over the form from Daphne when Elsie reaches us. "Can I come over?" Elsie asks.

"Sure," I say, hoping the combination of these two together will not make us all explode.

"Can I charge my phone while I'm here?" JennaLouise asks.

"You and all of Clay Coves," I say. The outlets in the strips on our driveway are almost all taken with phones charging, but there are two open on the end.

She plugs her phone in and then we walk through the garage to the basement, where Mom had put all the stuff that survived the flood on the table. I stop and tell Elsie, "JennaLouise's mom gave me a ton of stuff for that fundraiser I was thinking of doing, but this is all that survived the storm." And then I say to both of them, "Maybe you can help me sort through this and figure out which of these things to keep and which to toss? The things they weren't sure about. Would that be okay?"

Their agreement is wordless. JennaLouise grabs a laundry basket piled high with games and beach toys. "Upstairs?"

I nod and hand Elsie a couple of bailing buckets, mostly filled with cellophane and ribbons and the baskets that survived.

I grab the rest of the Daphne stuff and follow them upstairs.

Navy passes on his way to the garage. "Need some help?" he asks.

"Not now, but thanks." Since when does Navy help? What world is this?

We settle in the living room to examine each item to decide if it's in good enough shape to be put in a gift basket for an auction at Clay Coves Community Day, if that's what I end up doing. I won't know until we find out if Madison's dad is allergic, and the Chaplains said the only way is to bring Rigby to their house. And then once Irene says okay, I can officially get started on fundraising. My fingers are so crossed they hurt.

"This corkboard is still wet, but it's kind of cool," Jenna-Louise says.

"Does it smell?" Elsie asks.

"Excellent question," I say, reaching over and sniffing. "Smells like wet cork."

JennaLouise puts it in the maybe pile. And I kind of nod at the fact that there's a pile called maybe and it isn't killing me.

"So what have you been doing?" JennaLouise asks.

"Oh, helping my mom mostly," Elsie says. "She had some patients being boarded when the power went out and we had to set up a generator, but still, there was a lot of extra stuff to be done and so it's been really busy!"

JennaLouise watches Elsie the whole time she talks. "You are interesting, Elsie Jenkins," she finally says. I'm grateful she didn't say, *I wasn't asking* you.

"Thank you, but I prefer just Elsie."

JennaLouise smiles. "Got it. We all have our name issues," she says, turning to look at me, with my famously accidental name.

"So this pile is the stuff we can't use, right?" I ask. "Let's look through it one more time. I hate to lose so much. Your mother must be so annoyed with me."

"What?" JennaLouise says. "*No!* Not at all. She feels bad, actually. And she wants to help you. Really. She said she'll help you get set up at Clay Coves Community Day and she has ideas for what to do after that too, but you never told me why you need to raise money."

I tilt my head in the direction of Madison's house. "For that family. I'm trying to get them a service dog." I think of Rigby and the little black tip of his tail. But mostly I think about Band-Aid, *my* dog. When we got home Mom told Dad about the arrangement. Dad's a big dog lover. So even though it will be a lot of work, he said he'd be happy to do it.

JennaLouise and Elsie would be so happy if I told them I was getting a puppy—and that's kind of lucky, having friends who care like that. I can feel something like a seed almost sprouting, almost beginning to grow. Whatever the step before growth is. Maybe hope.

"But for now, on Friday, I'm going to be helping them on Fake Halloween. Well, I'm just going to be there so the dad can take Madison's baby brothers trick-or-treating, even though they're too young for it, really. Madison isn't going with them. I wish there was something I could do for her."

"You aren't trick-or-treating?" Elsie asks.

JennaLouise and I look at each other and I wish really hard that she won't say anything mean about outgrowing it. And she doesn't. "No," I say. "Not this year."

This year. This week! What an impossible week. The storm, the terrifying hunt for Madison, Irene's broken leg, Mr. Elkton and his white pickup truck hauling all those damaged and beat-up items away.

And I have an idea.

Almost as good as a magic dog.

Something that could make things better, possibly remove some danger from Madison's life.

"Do you know how I can reach Mr. Elkton?" I ask Elsie.

"Who?" JennaLouise asks.

"Johnny on the Spot. His name's Mr. Elkton. And he has something that . . . I don't want to say. I don't want to jinx it."

"Oh my God," JennaLouise says. "You've turned into your parents! Since when do you believe in jinxes?"

Ugh, she's right. I don't believe in jinxes, but I still don't want to say this out loud yet.

Elsie's hand reaches for the ring around her neck. Does she feel a pang when people mention parents? Or fathers? The way for a while I couldn't even think about dogs. I might once have been careful about this, making sure not to use the word *father* with Elsie. Instead, I make a note to do the opposite, to ask Elsie questions about him. To give her a new place in her life to remember him.

Elsie's hand lets go of the ring and she reaches for her phone. "My mom will know." She texts her mom and as we're passing around the corkboard to smell it one more time, Elsie gets a text back from her mother.

I grab my jacket and step outside to make the call. I take off one red mitten to dial the number.

"Johnny on the Spot!"

That's how he answers his phone? I laugh. "Hi. You don't know me I don't think, but you know my parents? The Morands? We—"

"Of course I know you. Hi, Army. What can I do for you?"

"A big favor," I say, "but it's not for me. Do you know the family that moved into the Rooneys' old house?"

"That little girl who was missing," he says.

"Yes, exactly. Well, I saw you hauling something, and if you wouldn't mind—" This is harder than I thought, asking him to give up something, even if it is for someone else. I'm not worried about sticking my nose where it doesn't belong anymore. That part, at least, feels right.

I reach for the growing nugget of courage inside me and tell him my idea.

CHAPTER THIRTY-SIX

I'm actually at Madison's house, explaining everything to Irene, when I get the text. We're talking about what a puppy could mean, and how if it doesn't work out—if the dad is allergic, if we can't raise enough money—Irene and her family are not obligated to keep the dog. I will still foster this puppy to be someone's service dog. And I really, really hope he's Madison's. But even if he's not, I'm giving it my best effort. And he led me to Band-Aid. Band-Aid, whose name quickly came to feel just right. Band-Aid. I can't change that name. It's what you use to heal the hurt. Band-Aid, who's coming home next week.

BRINGING IT OVER NOW.

That's what the text says. And I start laughing, because what is Elsie even talking about? I stare at it a few seconds, because something's not quite . . . It's not from Elsie. It's from Johnny on the Spot!

"And so there's just one more thing," I say with a smile.

I'm sure it's an embarrassed smile. Because when I pictured doing this for Madison, I somehow imagined it as a kind of private thing between Madison and me, almost like the secret way I used to bring Mr. Hoffart his newspaper. And as I think about what's going to happen in the next . . . whenever Johnny gets here, it's going to be just about the most public thing to ever go down on Marigold Street.

I have such a strong feeling that this is the right thing to do but I also know that Irene might veto it if I tell her. So I say, "I have a surprise planned for Madison," because it's true.

Irene laughs, which makes her leg hurt somehow, because she winces. "Really, Army? Something other than spearheading a huge neighborhood campaign to get her a magic hypoallergenic service dog?"

"Well, I was kind of worried about her *now*—like if Rigby works out, that'll be great, but Madison has to be okay until he's trained, and I think . . . I don't want to say any more. Could I ask you to stay inside and not look out the window, and keep Madison from doing the same? I'll get it ready, and then I'll show you both. Is that okay?"

She gives me this look like she knows she can't say no to that even though she might really want to. Before she has a chance, I go outside to wait for Johnny and I should have probably guessed this—when he pulls up, Elsie's sitting right there in the passenger seat. She climbs out and runs over to me, jumping up and down like it's Christmas morning and she's four.

"I'm gonna need a little help with this," Johnny calls out. "Can you find some folks to help?" He's untying the rope that's keeping his cargo from tipping right out of the bed of his truck.

The Hunts are walking toward us. "Need some help?" Mr. Hunt yells. I walk him over to the back of the truck—and then Linda and Sue seem to spot us from . . . where else, my driveway . . . and start jogging over to help with the unpacking and lifting.

I explain what I'm doing to Mrs. Hunt and she has the best idea. Elsie and I follow her to her backyard, where she shows us the trampoline pads no one is using now that their trampoline ran away from home and died a tragic public death in the storm.

"But are you getting a new trampoline? Won't you need them back then?"

Mrs. Hunt smiles. "Not to worry," she says. "Now that the kids are away at school, our trampoline days are over. Then she looks at me closely and says, "I've missed seeing you and your dog out every morning, Army. When I'd brew coffee for Ed and me, there you two would be, walking past my window. I was sorry to hear he died. He was a lovely dog."

Elsie grabs one of the pads and starts dragging it to Irene's house.

"Do you think you might get another dog sometime, sweetheart?"

It's the first time I say it out loud: "Yes. Next week. His name is Band-Aid." And I think about how I'll have Rigby for a while too. But I hope that he will be Madison's dog. Her magic dog.

It doesn't take long, with all the neighbors helping, to get it set up.

I go back into Madison's house, and she's standing right by the door, waiting for me. For this. We walk outside together and before I have a chance to explain it all to Irene, Madison walks straight to it and climbs as though she already knows where to find each foothold. As though she has been waiting for it. As though it is the very thing she has been waiting for. She perches on the broad wooden seat, where the lifeguards would sit, high above everything, safe and exactly where she needs to be. In front of her family's home, but up, high up. The mats are spread out below, around the base, in case Madison falls. But Madison won't fall.

Maybe she'll stay close to home—very close—now that there's a safe place to be up high right on her own front lawn.

EPILOGUE

High above streets lit by the warm dim glow of flashlights and lanterns, amid trees stripped of their leaves, sits a girl with a blond ponytail down her back. It is November and it is cold, but the little girl is wrapped in blankets. Below, parents watch from the sidewalk as their goblins and princesses and pirates and goons walk up to door after door, on the hunt for candy on this cold, dark night. The girl looks out beyond the alien, two bumblebees, the zombie hockey player. She's not looking at the neighbor girl sitting by the mailbox with a bowl of snack-size candy bars, but she knows she is there.

Down below, that girl is keeping a watchful eye and thinking about the pair of dogs who will soon arrive. One dog might be able to help the girl above, a new and steady force always by her side. And the other, a sweet tan ball of fluff with brown ears, has already started to heal her own broken heart.

The girl with a ponytail sits on this November evening, a belated Halloween, leans forward, and looks out at the dark night. Toward the low branches of trees. Up to the sky, to the moon, the stars, just beginning to glimmer in the blackness. The girl sits above it all—the laughs and shrieks and candy chaos—the neighborhood's sentry. Up here, all the way up here, on this night, all is well.

ACKNOWLEDGMENTS

I started this book more than six years ago. There have been so many helpful, supportive, loving, wise people along the way.

Liz Garton Scanlon was the first to read a raw, early version, and she did not cower. She did not vomit. In fact, she forced me to continue. She also offered up a cousin—which was easy for her to do, as she has hundreds.

Julie Manning (the cousin) allowed me to ask questions about her experiences with autism. I feel so lucky to have had her as a resource and for her willingness to read an early draft of this book. Her love and wisdom and pride inspired me. Katie Dersnah Mitchell is one of few superheroes who wears many hats. She donned them all when she read this book and offered wise insights and suggested ideas. I am forever grateful and also a little in awe. I would also like to thank one expert reader who was very generous with her experience as a psychologist and a neurodiverse individual, and who wishes not to be named here. Her eye-opening thoughts on this manuscript made it deeper, more authentic, and more sensitive. Any mistakes in my portrayal of Madison, a fictional character with nonverbal autism, are entirely my own.

Erin Murphy, my agent, helped me find the heart of the story, which is no surprise from such a big-hearted person.

Margaret Ferguson, my editor, has led me through an amazing and much-appreciated master class on editing and revision. (And I may have taught her a thing or two about jinxes along the way.)

Also, at Holiday House, big thanks to Mary Cash, Terry Borzumato-Greenberg, and Nicole Benevento. Also thanks to Chandra Wohleber, who worked hard to keep Army from sounding like a 38-year-old woman.

Patti Gauch pushed me to write deeper and to just say it! Writers have many voices clamoring for attention in their brain. I'm glad Patti's is one of the loud ones in mine.

Michael, Jacob, and Anna put up with a wife/mother who takes more than six years to write a novel, and never rolled their eyes or asked when I'd be done. And I could never do anything without my sisters, Beth Arnold and Ellen Gidaro. Obviously.

I am so grateful for my dear writer friends who read and shared thoughts and held my hand when necessary, most especially Olugbemisola Rhuday-Perkovich and Kimberly Marcus.

I would also like to thank the New Jersey Arts Council for support throughout the years.

When I learned that this book had found a home at

Margaret Ferguson Books, I was on vacation with 26 of my nearest and dearest. Some, perhaps those who believe in jinxes and the opposite of jinxes, might think it would be fortuitous to gather three generations of the family together again. So, Jules and Barbara Glassman and your 24 other nearest and dearest, what do you think?